"I couldn't . . .
she gasped. "I wanted to...

"I wanted to kill Midnight for destroying Frank. And I wanted Virgil Gates to find the body. I wanted him to know that he hadn't won." Her hands clenched on Matt's chest.

"But I couldn't do it."

Matt's arms tightened around her. She was so wounded and alone. Her vulnerability tore at his heart. His protective instincts surged. He found himself wanting to fight her battles and keep her from harm. Without conscious thought he let his lips nibble along her hairline, tasting the sweetness of her skin.

For a moment her breath seemed to stop. She gave a tremulous little sigh and began to melt against him. Then, abruptly, she stiffened in his arms. Bracing her hands against his chest, she shoved him away. Shards of ice glittered in her violet eyes.

"Maybe I should have shot *you* instead," she said coldly.

* * *

Wyoming Wildfire

Harlequin® Historical #792—March 2006

Acclaim for Elizabeth Lane

Her Dearest Enemy
"A pleasurable and well-executed tale."
—*Romantic Times BOOKclub*

Wyoming Woman
"This credible, now-or-never romance moves with reckless speed through a highly engrossing and compact plot to the kind of happy ending we read romances to enjoy."
—*Romantic Times BOOKclub*

Bride On the Run
"Enjoyable and satisfying all round, BRIDE ON THE RUN is an excellent Western romance you won't want to miss!"
—*Romance Reviews Today*

Apache Fire
"Enemies, lovers, raw passion, taut sexual tension, murder and revenge—Indian romance fans are in for a treat with Elizabeth Lane's sizzling tale of forbidden love."
—*Romantic Times BOOKclub*

ELIZABETH LANE

WYOMING WILDFIRE

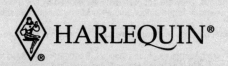

HARLEQUIN®

TORONTO • NEW YORK • LONDON
AMSTERDAM • PARIS • SYDNEY • HAMBURG
STOCKHOLM • ATHENS • TOKYO • MILAN • MADRID
PRAGUE • WARSAW • BUDAPEST • AUCKLAND

ISBN 0-373-29392-5

WYOMING WILDFIRE

Please address questions and book requests to:
Harlequin Reader Service
U.S.: 3010 Walden Ave., P.O. Box 1325, Buffalo, NY 14269
Canadian: P.O. Box 609, Fort Erie, Ont. L2A 5X3

For Powderpuff,
Who left her pawprints on my heart
1982–2005

Chapter One

Felton, Wyoming,
May, 1887

Jessie Hammond belly-crawled her way up the muddy bank that rose above the wagon road. Her right hand clawed for purchase on the rain-soaked ground. Her left hand gripped the handle of a long-barreled Colt Peacemaker. The hefty single-action revolver was loaded and Jessie knew how to use it. Only last week, she'd downed a prime buck at a hundred yards with a shot through the heart. But she didn't intend to fire the weapon today. Not unless she had to.

Digging into the mud with the toes of her worn riding boots, she heaved her way onto the level ground at the crest of the bank. Keeping low, she inched forward through the rabbit brush to the edge, where the ground dropped off fifteen feet to the road below. She anxiously scanned the road's rutted surface.

Last night's storm had flooded the wagon tracks and turned the indentations to gleaming puddles. Fresh hoofprints would be easy to spot because they wouldn't be filled with water. Jessie saw none. Unless the lawman had chosen to take her brother the twenty miles to Sheridan by a different route, she had managed to arrive here ahead of them.

Jessie had watched from behind the Felton general store that morning as Heber Sims, the elderly town marshal, had opened up the makeshift jailhouse and allowed the tall U.S. deputy to lead the manacled prisoner to the spare horse. Jessie knew that Heber would be relieved to see Frank gone. There'd been talk of a lynching, and if a mob had stormed the jail, neither the old man nor the rickety clapboard building would have been strong enough to stop them.

As the two men were mounting up, Jessie had sprinted for her own horse, sneaked quietly out of hearing, and then cut hell for leather across the open hills to intercept them on the road. It was a desperate risk she was taking, but she had to stop the federal deputy from locking Frank up in Sheridan. She had to convince him of the truth—that her brother was innocent of murdering Allister Gates.

The Gates brothers' ranch occupied a choice

spread of land bordering upper Goose Creek. While not as wealthy as the Tollivers, who owned the vast acreage to the north, the family was certainly well-off. Allister, a big, affable man in his early fifties, had looked after the ranch's financial interests while Virgil, a decade younger, ramrodded the work.

Allister had been well-thought-of by the townspeople and neighboring ranchers. The whole community had been thrown into shock two nights ago by the discovery of his body, sprawled facedown in the horse corral owned by the Gates with a bullet through the back. Frank's rifle, with his initials, F.H., carved into the stock, had been found lying a few feet away.

Marshal Sims, flanked by two nervous deputies, had come for Frank just as he and Jessie were finishing breakfast the next morning. They had clapped the handcuffs around Frank's wrists, giving him no time to resist.

"Since when is it a crime for a man to steal back his own horse?" Frank had argued as they led him toward the marshal's buggy. "Far as I'm concerned, it's Allister Gates you should be arresting, not me."

Only then had the marshal told Frank that he was under arrest for Allister's murder.

Frank's young face had turned as white as bleached bone. "No!" he'd screamed as the deputies dragged him into the buggy. "I only took the stallion! Allister made me drop my gun, and I rode off without getting it back, but the man was alive when I left the place! I swear it by all that's holy! On my parents' graves, I swear I didn't kill him!" His frantic gaze had swung toward Jessie, who stood frozen in shock. "Help me, sis! Tell them! Make them listen!"

The memory of his cries tore at Jessie's heart as she crouched in the tall brush, waiting. What she was about to do would likely get her arrested, too. But once Frank was locked up in Sheridan, she would be all but helpless to aid him. With the evidence that stood against him, he could be tried and hanged in a matter of days, giving her no time to clear his name. She had to act now, before it was too late.

A spring breeze skimmed her face, fluttering one jet-black curl that had tumbled loose from beneath her old felt hat. Nervously she tucked it back beneath the brim. She'd disguised herself as a boy because she didn't want to be recognized. But she'd begun to wonder how well her masquerade would work. Even with her hair out of sight, she didn't look much like a male. The bandanna over her face would help a little, as would the baggy flannel shirt and muddy bib overalls she wore, but making her voice sound convincing would be more difficult.

Clearing her throat, she rehearsed the words she'd planned to say. "Unbuckle your gun belt, Marshal, and throw it up to me. Do it nice and easy, and you won't get hurt. Now, unlock those handcuffs, and…"

Jessie sighed and shook her head. She sounded like an actress filling in for the villain in a bad melodrama. She wouldn't need a gun. The marshal would likely be overcome by helpless laughter.

But this was no laughing matter, she reminded herself. And it was too late to change her plans now. She could hear the sound of horses coming up the road from the south. A moment later, two mounted figures, riding side by side with a loose rope connecting their saddles, appeared around the bend in the road.

Frank sat astride a docile-looking bay. His head was bare and his hands were manacled behind his back. He looked rumpled, unshaven and terrified. He was nineteen years old, with his whole life ahead of him. Right now that precious life lay in Jessie's hands.

The deputy marshal, who moved along beside him on a classy, long-legged chestnut, was a stranger. Like the horse he rode, he was lean, athletic and ruggedly handsome. His eyes were narrowed and alert beneath the brim of his Stetson. His hand rested lightly on the grip of his holstered revolver. The six-point silver star of his office gleamed on his leather vest. Studying him, Jessie could sense the tension that fueled his steel spring reflexes. Such a man would be hard to take by surprise. But surprise was essential if her plan were to succeed.

Jessie pulled the bandanna over the lower part of her face. She would wait until they'd passed her hiding place. That would put her at the marshal's back, giving her a slight advantage when she made her move. What happened after that would be anybody's guess. But if Frank got away unharmed, she would count it as a victory.

As she crept toward the edge of the bank her index finger settled against the familiar steel curve of the Peacemaker's trigger. Her thumb eased the hammer back into firing position. She didn't want to hurt the deputy, but she would do whatever it took to rescue her brother. She could only pray that, when the time came, the lawman would listen to reason.

United States Deputy Marshal Matthew T. Langtry cast a sidelong glance at his prisoner. Frank Hammond didn't strike him as a killer. The poor devil was painfully young and scared spitless. What was more, he didn't appear to have a mean bone in his body. Bringing in vicious lawbreakers generally gave Matt a sense of satisfaction. He felt no such satisfaction this morning, only an uneasy premonition that something wasn't right.

The aging town marshal had given Matt the facts of the case. Frank Hammond and Allister Gates had been at odds over the ownership of a valuable horse. Gates had taken custody of the horse and put it in his corral. Late in the night, young Hammond had come to steal the horse back. Gates had tried to stop him, but somehow Hammond had escaped with the horse and vanished into the darkness. Gates had been found in the corral, shot in the back. The bullet, cut from his body by the undertaker, was matched to Hammond's rifle, which had been left at the scene.

A tidy little story, Matt mused. Almost too tidy. But that was none of his affair. This wasn't even his blasted case. Newly arrived at his own post in Sheridan, he'd been paying a courtesy call on Johnson County Sheriff Frank Canton, when word came in that a prisoner needed to be brought in from Felton. Being new to the area and wanting to see more of the country, Matt had offered to go.

All he needed to do now was deliver Frank Hammond to the jail in Sheridan and hand over the legal paperwork. Then he could get back to the paperwork that had piled up on his own desk. Hellfire, if he'd known that working for the federal government involved so damned much paper, he'd have thought twice before taking the job.

But this murder case…against his better judgment, it was pulling him in. The Felton marshal's story had left a lot of holes to fill. For example…

"Where's the horse you stole, Frank?" he asked, thinking aloud. "The stallion?"

"Hid." Frank's blue eyes flashed beneath his thick,

black brows. "And I didn't steal him. He's mine, bought and paid for. My sister's got the bill of sale at home. She can show it to you."

"Your sister?"

"Jessie. We've got a homestead back in the hills. The two of us have worked it since our folks died four years ago. Land's too poor for crops, so we breed and break horses. We were betting everything we had on that stallion and the colts he could sire. Allister Gates had no right to take him!"

"Did you kill Allister?" Matt's gaze drilled into the pupils of Frank's bloodshot eyes, probing for the truth.

"No!" Frank shook his head vehemently. "I swear it by the Almighty, I'd never—"

"Stop right there, Marshal. Unfasten that gun belt and throw it up here!" The throaty voice rasped out from behind and above them, on the high bank.

Matt swore under his breath. One glance at Frank Hammond's transfixed, hopeful face was enough to give Matt a fair idea of who was up there; and the faked masculine snarl bore out his suspicions. He knew a woman's voice when he heard one.

His hand tensed on the grip of his holstered Smith & Wesson .44. He could turn swiftly and hope to get the drop on her. But that would be a risky proposition, and he sure as hell didn't want to end up shooting her.

"I said take off that gun belt, Marshal." The husky,

oddly sensual voice was raw with strain. "I've got your back in my sights, and at this range I never miss!"

Matt decided to gamble. "Don't be a fool, Jessie," he said. "If you want to save your brother, let me take him in. I'll do everything I can to make sure he gets a fair—"

The report of the six-shooter exploded in Matt's ears, blasting the Stetson off his head. He sat stunned, his ears ringing. The hellcat wasn't bluffing. She could shoot.

"Mind what I say, or the next bullet will be lower." She was speaking in a flat, cold tone now, making no effort to disguise her voice. "Toss the gun belt up here. Then climb down off your horse."

Again Matt chose to stall. "You've already broken the law, Jessie—aiding a fugitive, assaulting a federal officer and Lord knows what else. You can't help your brother if you're in jail. Back off now, before anybody gets hurt, and I'm willing to forget what you've—"

"Just do it." He heard the click as she thumbed back the hammer. "I don't want to shoot you, Marshal, but I'd rather spill your blood than see my brother hang for a murder he didn't commit."

"If he runs, nobody will ever believe he's innocent."

"They don't believe it now. Half the town is out to lynch him—and I'll bet money the judge in Sheridan won't believe him, either. This is the only way.

Now, toss me the gun belt before you make us both sorry."

Frank cleared his throat. "Better do as she says, Marshal. Jessie's got a mean temper, and she's a helluva good shot."

Matt's curses purpled the air as he unbuckled the gun belt. He didn't like being bested by anyone, let alone a female. This incident would go on his record and make him the butt of some merciless ribbing. But he didn't want to shoot either of these young people. And he sure as blazes didn't want to get shot himself.

The belt and holster fell free. Turning toward the high, brushy bank, he swung it back and tossed it upward. The throw was short, as Matt had intended it to be. It bounced off the high slope of the bank and dropped into the sludge that the storm had washed along the road's lower edge. The last thing he wanted was to make it easy for her.

The rabbit brush moved as she rose to her feet, giving him his first good look at her. If it hadn't been for the sight of the cocked Peacemaker pointing straight at his chest, he might have smiled, or even chuckled. By now he knew better.

She was a little thing, not a shade over five foot one. Aside from that, he could see almost nothing of Jessie Hammond. A battered old felt hat hid her hair and forehead, and the lower part of her face was masked by a crimson bandanna. Whatever figure she might possess was lost beneath a faded flannel shirt and a baggy, mud-streaked pair of bib overalls. Something about her reminded him of a little girl playing dress-up in her grandfather's old work clothes. But there was nothing make-believe about the cocked pistol in her hand.

"That wasn't funny." She jerked her head toward Matt's gun belt, which was already settling into the ooze. "I ought to shoot you right now."

"I can get it for you." Matt squinted up at her, wondering whether the black powder bullets in his pistol would be too wet to fire by the time he got his hands on the gun. He'd hoped she might make the mistake of climbing down to the road, but she stayed above him, keeping the advantage.

"Never mind. Get off your horse."

"Yes, ma'am." Matt eased out of the saddle and dropped to the ground.

"Now get your key and unlock my brother's handcuffs."

"Sorry. The key's hooked to the gun belt." It wasn't true, but it gave him an excuse to stall while he plotted his next move. Strangely enough, he'd begun to enjoy this little sparring match.

"He's lying, sis," Frank said. "I saw the tricky bastard put the key in his pocket."

Her eyes flashed above the red bandanna. Even at a distance, Matt could see that they were the color of violets, almost purple, and framed with luxuriant ebony lashes. "Don't play games with me, Marshal!" she snapped. "I'm running out of patience, and my trigger finger's getting itchier by the minute!"

"Whatever you say, lady." Matt fumbled in his pocket, thinking that he'd give a new saddle and his Sunday hat to know what was underneath that silly costume of hers. If the rest of Jessie Hammond matched those eyes…Lord Almighty!

His fingers found the small key and the ring that held it. Still he hesitated, stalling as he searched for some way to salvage this debacle.

He glanced up at Jessie, then back at her brother. "You know, Frank, if you ride out of here, you'll have a whole troop of vigilantes on your trail. And if they find you before the law does, you'll be swinging on a rope before you can say your prayers."

"I'll be swinging anyway," Frank muttered. "At least, if I run, I'll have a fighting chance. Do what she says, Marshal."

Matt sighed as he pulled the keys out of his pocket. "I just wish you'd—"

The rest of the sentence died in his throat as he sensed a slight tremor in the mud beneath his boots and heard, from beyond the bend in the road, the rumble of galloping horses—many horses—coming from the direction of the town. Matt's instincts slammed into high alert. Only one thing would bring a large band of riders onto the road this morning.

"Vigilantes!" Frank's face had gone chalky. Still handcuffed, he leaned forward in the saddle and, gripping with his knees, jabbed his boots into the side of the horse he was riding. The startled bay shot off the road and up the hill, with Frank clinging Indian-style to its back.

Roped to the other horse's saddle, Copper, Matt's chestnut gelding was yanked into motion. Copper snorted, jumped, and broke into a gallop, keeping even with the bay. Matt swore as his prisoner and both horses vanished over the top of the wooded ridge. He could hear the riders approaching the bend in the road. Seconds from now they would be in sight.

Jessie stood on the high bank, her pistol arm hanging slack as she stared after her brother.

"Get out of here, damn it!" Matt snapped, lunging for his gun. "You're the last person I want those hotheaded fools to find!"

He found the gun belt in the muddy roadside ditch and jerked his pistol out of the holster. When he looked up again, Jessie Hammond had disappeared behind the top of the bank. He hoped she'd have the good sense to run. If the vigilantes failed to find Frank, they could turn their fury on his sister. Whatever happened after that was bound to be ugly.

He took a split second to examine the gun. The

leather had kept the weapon relatively clean of mud, but it hadn't kept out the moisture. There was no way of knowing whether the bullets would fire except to pull the trigger, and there was no time for that. Any second now, the riders would be thundering around the bend—and right now he had a fast decision to make.

The high-minded course of action would be to face them down and use his authority as a federal marshal to turn them back. But when the vigilantes saw him on foot, without his prisoner, they'd likely guess what had happened. If they picked up Frank Hammond's trail, they'd be off like a herd of banshees and Frank would be as good as dead.

If, on the other hand, he took the coward's way out and hid, they might gallop right on past, thinking he and Frank were ahead of them on the road. With luck, they'd ride all the way to Sheridan, break up and head for the saloons to cool their thirst. That would give him time to round up Frank and bring him in by another route.

There were times when cowardice made more sense than bravery. This was one of them.

The riders were getting close. With a hasty glance toward the bend in the road, Matt clawed his way up the steep bank, dived between two clumps of rabbit brush and tumbled headlong over the top.

Chapter Two

A grunt of surprise exploded between Matt's lips as his body collided with something soft and yielding. His pulse slammed, but before he could right himself and look around, he felt the cold jab of a muzzle between his ribs.

"Lay one finger on me, Marshal, and I'll blow you to kingdom come!" The voice was so close that he could feel the warm breath in his ear. Matt muttered a few choice words no lady should ever hear—but then he'd seen no evidence that Jessie Hammond was any kind of lady.

"I thought I told you to get out of here!" he growled.

"I'll get out of here when I'm ready. Right now, I need to see what's happening."

"Then put that damned gun away before it goes off. Believe me, I wouldn't lay a finger on you for a month of paydays." Matt could hear the riders coming closer. The last thing he needed now was for this trigger-happy hellion to start more trouble.

Moving cautiously, he eased himself away from the steely pressure of the gun. She made no move to stop him as he inched toward the top of the bank. "Stay where you are and keep still," he hissed.

Instead of obeying, she crawled up alongside him. "I want to see, too," she whispered through the bandanna that still covered most of her face. "You won't recognize the rotten skunks. I will."

He couldn't argue with that, Matt conceded. But even if he'd chosen to, there was no more time. He heard her breath catch as the band of mounted vigilantes exploded around the bend in the road. There were about twenty riders, he calculated, all of them masked, armed and, from the looks of them, well fortified with whiskey. Why they'd waited this long to come after Frank instead of busting down the jail was anybody's guess. Maybe they thought there'd be too many witness in town.

Behind those drawn-up neckerchiefs were the faces of farmers, ranchers, hired hands and townspeople—husbands, sons and fathers. Half of them would be scared to death, Matt reminded himself. But even the most law-abiding citizens could be swept away by the violent madness of a lynch mob.

In their present condition these men were as dangerous as a pack of rabid dogs.

"The brute in the lead is Virgil Gates, Allister's
brother," Jessie whispered, close to his ear. "I'd know
that big, ugly piebald horse of his anywhere. And I
can pick out a half-dozen of the cowhands who work
on his ranch, and a few no-accounts from town who'd
ride anywhere for a bottle. The rest of them are likely
from other ranches around here. I don't—"

"Shh!" Matt hushed her with a jab of his elbow.
His heart froze as he realized the riders were slowing down, most likely to let some stragglers catch up.
He'd been hoping—almost expecting—they would
just ride on down the main road. If they stopped here,
there was a real danger they'd notice the trail of fresh
hoofprints where Frank had fled up the hill with the
horses.

The bullnecked man Jessie had identified as Virgil Gates reined in his horse. Matt held his breath as
Gates lowered his mask, pulled a silver whiskey flask
out of his pocket and raised it to his mouth. A few of
those with him did the same. It took a lot of liquid
courage to hang a man.

Jessie wriggled upward, trying to see. Fearing she
might move too far or loosen a rock, Matt grabbed
the seat of her overalls and held her down. She
squirmed against his fist. Blast the woman. He could
have managed fine without her interference.

Time crawled as Virgil Gates stoppered the flask, shoved it into his pocket, wiped his mouth on the back of his hands and adjusted the thick coil of rope that lay over his saddle horn. "Let's go, boys," he said, motioning with his arm.

Jerking his mask into place, he spurred the big piebald to a gallop and headed down the road toward Sheridan. The rest of the mob thundered after him in grim silence, as if weighed down by the awful thing they'd set out to do.

Dizzy with relief, Matt watched them go. With luck, they'd be miles away before they realized their quarry wasn't ahead of them. For now, at least, he was free to deal with other problems.

He groaned out loud as he felt the thrust of Jessie Hammond's pistol against his ribs once more. "What the hell—"

"I want the key, Marshal." Her breathy voice rasped in his ear. "The key to the handcuffs. Give it to me now, and you'll be free to walk back to Felton."

"And if I don't?" Matt stalled, knowing he had to beat her at her own game. If Jessie was demanding the key, she likely knew where Frank was headed. More important, she almost certainly had a horse hidden nearby—a horse he needed.

"You can give me the key now, or I can take it off your dead body. It's all the same to me."

Matt sighed. "You're not much of a bluffer, Jessie.

If you were capable of murdering me, you'd have done it by now."

"You don't know that for sure. And I wouldn't have to kill you. I could hurt you so badly that you'd wish you were dead."

"One shot would bring those vigilantes right back here."

"Not fast enough to catch me. Now stop dithering and give me that key!" The Peacemaker jabbed harder against his ribs.

"You know where it is." Matt's muscles tensed like coiled springs. "If you want the key, just reach into my pocket and get it. Go on."

Caught off guard, she shifted against him to reach the pocket. For the space of a heartbeat she was vulnerable. That was all the time Matt needed.

Twisting sharply, he made his move. His body exploded upward, hands flashing to catch her wrists. She gave a little cry as the force of his weight struck her, flipping her sideways onto her back, with his weight above her.

She lay on her back, glaring up at him with those deep lilac eyes. Her hat had tumbled off, revealing a spill of night-black curls, but the bandanna remained in place over her nose and mouth. "Get off me!" she sputtered. "Let go of me now, or I'll scream!"

"Go ahead." Using his weight to pin her against the slope, he locked one hand around her wrists while his other hand pried the Peacemaker from her fingers. To control her hands, he had to straddle her impossibly tiny waist with his knees and lean forward. The body beneath him felt small but voluptuous through the baggy denim overalls. The pressure of her jutting breasts against his belly sent waves of erotic awareness ripping down into his loins. To his chagrin, Matt realized he was fully aroused. He swore under his breath, hoping she wouldn't feel him against her and get the wrong idea. He liked his ladies in satin and perfume—more important, he liked them willing. And right now, the only things he wanted from Jessie Hammond were her gun, her horse and her cooperation.

She had stopped struggling and gone rigid beneath him. She knew, all right—probably wanted to kill him for what he couldn't help. The sooner he got off her the better. But there was one temptation, heaven save him, that Matt was unable to resist.

He had to see that face.

Releasing the hammer on the Peacemaker, Matt thrust it into his belt. Then, still pinioning her wrists, he used his free hand to tug away the red bandanna, revealing the lower part of her face.

He stifled a reflexive gasp.

If Frank Hammond's sister had been as plain as mud, he thought, it would have made everything easier. But she was far from plain. And as Matt filled his gaze with the sight of her heart-shaped face, lush lips and straight little nose, crowned by those unearthly violet eyes, he knew that he was in danger of tumbling over the edge of reason. The heavenly powers were too prudent to have created such a face—only the devil could have done it.

"Let me up." Her whispery voice raked his senses. "No tricks, I promise, as long as you agree to listen to my story."

"You can tell me your story while we ride after your brother." Matt sat back on his heels. "Come on. Let's go."

She'd begun to struggle again. "But I haven't got—"

"Don't lie to me, Jessie. You and your brother raise horses—that's what he told me. And you didn't get clear out here on foot. Now take me to your horse. We can ride double till we come up with something better."

Rising, he jerked her none too gently to her feet. She was the sister of an accused killer, desperate to free her brother, he reminded himself. To save Frank Hammond's life, she would lie, steal, seduce—and maybe even put a bullet through an unwary lawman's heart. Show even a moment's weakness, and she would pounce on it like a cat. He could not afford to lower his guard, even for an instant.

"Where's the horse?" His grip tightened on her arm, easing only when she winced and pointed downhill toward a wash, where willows trailed over a sluggish stream.

"What are you going to do?" She stumbled over her boots as he pulled her roughly down the hill.

"I'm going to find your brother, make certain he's safe, and take him to Sheridan for trial. That's my job. If I want to keep it, I have no choice."

"What if I could prove to you that Frank didn't kill Allister Gates?" She stumbled, twisting her ankle as she went down on one knee. Matt forced himself to keep moving, dragging her along until she regained her footing.

"Can you prove it?"

"I could try! That's more than you've done!" She wrenched herself loose and stood facing him, her raven hair bannering in the wind. "Look at the facts! Frank dropped the rifle. Anybody could've picked it up and used it to shoot Allister!"

"I'd wager that's exactly what his lawyer will argue. Reasonable doubt." He seized her arm again, yanking her against his side as he strode down the grassy hillside. "It's a fair defense and it might work. But I won't be on the bench or in the jury box. My only duty is to bring him in."

"You're heartless!" She flung the words at him. "Frank's never harmed a soul in his life! Why, *I'm* more capable of killing Allister Gates than he is."

"Now that I can believe." Matt cast her a sidelong

glance and was seared by the blaze of fury in her eyes. "I have to ask," he said. "Did you kill him?"

"Of course not! And neither did Frank!"

"So who did? You must have given the answer some thought."

She frowned, the black wings of her eyebrows shifting pensively. "It had to be someone at the ranch, someone who was close enough to see the rifle and seize the chance to kill Allister before he went back into the house…maybe a cowhand with a grudge, or even Virgil. He had the most to gain from his brother's death."

"But you have no proof."

"No. No more proof than you have against Frank."

They had reached the stand of tall willows where Jessie had tethered the horse, a sleek buckskin mare that nickered and pricked its ears at their approach. It was a beautiful, spirited animal, Matt thought, not unlike its owner. But Jessie Hammond had too much spirit for her own good. From the moment he'd first heard her voice, the woman had caused him nothing but trouble. He'd be crazy to take her with him when he could just as easily trail Frank on his own.

For the space of a breath he weighed the idea of leaving her behind. It was a tempting notion—he would have no trouble following the horses' tracks without her. But no, he concluded, he needed her with him. She could tell him things he needed to know, and if it came to a showdown with Frank, she might prove useful—providing he could keep the little hellion under control.

Deciding to test her, he released her arm and turned to free the mare's tether. "I've decided not to take you with me. You can walk back to town from here and find a way home. When I get my own horse back, I'll see that this one is returned to you."

"No!" The word exploded out of her. "I don't care if you *are* a lawman, I won't let you take Gypsy without me! And I need to be there when you find Frank. He'll be scared. He could even be hurt! I've always been there to look out for him. I can't fail him now!"

Even after what he'd already experienced, Matt was startled by her vehemence. And the fact that she'd looked out for Frank was a revelation. He'd assumed, perhaps because of her diminutive size, that she was younger than Frank. Now, studying her determined features, he realized she must be in her early twenties—a fiercely protective older sister.

"Take me with you!" she insisted, seizing Matt's arm. "You need to understand what's happened and why Frank has to be innocent. I can tell you everything. Please—I promise not to give you any more trouble!"

He'd believe that when pigs could fly, Matt thought. But at least it was a step in the right direction. "You can ride behind me. If you go for the gun or the key or try any other tricks, you'll find yourself on the ground. Understand?"

She nodded. "I don't believe we've been properly introduced. You know my name, but I don't know yours."

He inclined his head in a mocking bow. "Deputy Marshal Matthew T. Langtry, at your service, ma'am."

"And I suppose the *T* stands for Texas. I could butter a biscuit with that drawl of yours, Marshal."

"Whatever you say." Matt swung into the saddle, hoping she would dismiss the subject of his name. But as he reached down to pull her up behind him, she probed deeper.

"Now you've got me curious. What does the *T* really stand for?" Her husky voice had taken on a teasing note. "Thadeus? Terwilliger?"

Matt sighed. "Close. It's Tolliver."

"Oh?" She settled herself into place behind the saddle, her hands resting lightly against his ribs. "Are you related to the Tollivers who live north of here? The ones who own the biggest spread in the county?"

"Being from Texas, I don't rightly know." Matt nudged the mare to a silky-smooth canter. He'd been asked the same question before and had given the same answer. He'd done enough quiet checking to know that the late Jacob Tolliver, who'd founded the ranch a generation ago, had brought most of his cattle up from Texas. Jacob had left the place to his sons, Morgan, who was half Shoshone, and Ryan, who'd recently sold out his share and moved to the Canadian border.

Matt knew little else about the family except that they were well respected. He wasn't sure he wanted to know more, or to know them. And the very last thing he'd ever want to do would be to ride onto the Tolliver ranch, knock on Morgan Tolliver's front door and announce, *You don't know me, but I have reason to believe I might be your long-lost bastard half brother!*

Especially when he could be wrong.

But never mind the Tollivers. Right now he had his hands full with an escaped prisoner, a liquored-up lynch mob and an unpredictable hellion who'd do anything to save her brother. It was up to him to keep all hell from breaking loose.

Spurring the mare to a gallop, he cut off the main road and headed for the ridge where Frank Hammond had disappeared.

Chapter Three

⤜⤛⤐⤐⤐⤐⤐⤑⤑

Jessie clung to Matt Langtry's waist, leaning outward to see past his broad shoulders. They had followed Frank's trail over the first ridge and up the long slope into the high brush. The going was slower here, with the trail obscured by thickets of scrub oak and big-tooth maple, dotted higher up with pale stands of aspen.

It didn't take a skilled tracker to see that the two horses had been out of control when they'd passed this way. In spots where the trail was clear, the brush was broken and trampled, the earth scarred with the prints of galloping hooves. Frank was an expert rider, but with his hands manacled behind his back, he would be able to do little more than cling to the horse with his knees. He could easily be thrown, or worse, caught by a stirrup and dragged over the rocky ground. The thought of what could happen triggered a spasm of horror in the pit of Jessie's stomach.

But she couldn't help Frank by worrying, she reminded herself. Her best chance of getting him out of this mess now lay in pleading his case to Matt Langtry. If she could make the tall federal deputy see the truth, or even win his sympathy, he might be persuaded to help her find out who'd really killed Allister Gates. But how persuadable would Matthew Tolliver Langtry be?

If she'd met him under different circumstances—at a dance, say, or a church supper—she might have been drawn to his chiseled features, gold-flecked brown eyes and rangy, athletic body. She might have flirted a little, laughing and tossing her hair, wanting to catch his eye, wanting him to smile and walk her way. Wanting him to reach out and touch her.

Even now, where her nipples brushed the back of his leather vest, the awareness of his body was like a subtle electric current that tingled along her nerves, pulsing deep and hot where her thighs nested against his long legs. It might be possible to imagine more, or even to make it happen. But Jessie's actual experience with the male sex had been limited to a few groping kisses from eager farm boys—kisses from which she'd always pulled away feeling flustered and ashamed. She was anything but an accomplished seductress. Trying to charm a man like Matt Langtry with her scant feminine wiles would only make her look like a fool.

Matt was a man intent on his job, and there was only one weapon in her meager arsenal that had any chance of moving him.

That weapon was the truth.

"You have to believe my brother is innocent," she said, plunging to the heart of the matter. "I've known Frank all his life. He could never have murdered Allister Gates."

"I know you'd like to believe that." Matt guided the mare around a clump of juniper, his eyes scanning the ground. "But you can't know for certain unless you were there."

"I *was* there!"

Jessie felt his body jerk against her. To his way of thinking, she'd likely made herself an accessory to horse stealing and possible murder. But never mind that. She would do whatever it took to save her brother.

"Oh, I don't mean *right* there," she added hastily. "But I was close by. Frank and I rode Gypsy as far as the Goose Creek ford, about a quarter mile from the Gates house. After we crossed, I let him off so he could go in on foot and get Midnight—the stallion. Then I waited for him, maybe twenty minutes, before I heard him coming back."

"Did you hear anything else?" Matt Langtry's voice was flat and tough, the voice of a lawman questioning a suspect.

"Not voices. I was too far away for that. But I would have heard a gunshot. I was listening the whole time, and I *didn't* hear one. Allister wasn't shot until some time after my brother left him. I'd swear to that on a stack of Bibles!"

"Go on," he said, his tone betraying nothing.

"We rode hard and didn't get a chance to talk until we were in the hills. That was when Frank told me that Allister had come out to the corral and caught him leading Midnight from the barn. Allister had a pistol, and he ordered Frank to throw down the rifle. Frank did, but before Allister could pick the rifle up, Midnight reared and struck him in the head. Allister went down. Frank said he was groaning and moving, so he couldn't have been too badly hurt."

"So Frank just jumped on the stallion and galloped away?"

"That's right. He didn't realize he'd forgotten the rifle until I asked him what had happened to it."

"Why did he take the rifle in the first place?" Matt's question was sharp, almost contemptuous.

"For protection, of course! Frank would never set out to harm anyone!" Jessie battled the urge to shout at the man and pummel his back with her fists. Why did he seem so determined to believe in Frank's guilt? Was it because that belief made his job simpler and eased his own conscience?

"Don't you understand?" she exploded. "I waited and listened the whole time Frank was gone! There was no gunshot!"

"Would you be willing to swear to that in court?" His question chilled her.

"Certainly. It's the truth."

"Is it, Jessie? Do you think the jury will believe a sister who'd do anything, even perjure herself, to save her brother's life?"

Jessie swallowed the bitter taste of her own fear. "Right now, the important thing is, do *you* believe me."

He didn't reply.

Jessie sank into an uneasy silence as they wound their way up the slope. The sun shone high and bright in a cloudless sky, and the aspens wore baby leaves, small and pale and new. A scrub jay scolded from the top of an ancient pine tree. It would have been a beautiful day, Jessie thought, except for the worry that blackened her spirits, casting its pall over everything she saw.

What if Matt Langtry insisted on taking Frank in? How could she stop him?

Each idea that came to mind seemed more ludicrous than the last. But one thing was certain—whatever it took, she had to stop the marshal from taking her brother in to Sheridan. If she failed, Frank would never make it home alive.

"Tell me about the stallion," Matt Langtry said,

breaking the silence. "Why were your brother and Allister Gates fighting in the first place?"

"Midnight is a full-blooded Arabian," Jessie said, thinking how their purchase of the fiery, pitch-black animal had set loose a deluge of bad luck. "We found him almost a year ago through a newspaper advertisement. The owner had lost all his money and had to sell out his stables. Frank mortgaged the ranch for the cash to buy the stallion and ship him by rail from Kentucky. We were hoping to make good money racing him in Sheridan, putting him out to stud, and then later selling his colts from our mares."

"I take it things didn't work out that way."

"No." Jessie suppressed a sigh. She'd tried to talk Frank out of buying the stallion, but her brother had set his heart on having the beautiful horse, and in the end she'd gone along.

"It was almost as if the horse was cursed," she said. "We had one delay after another. First the papers were lost in the mail. Then Frank came down with scarlet fever and was too sick to go to Kentucky and fetch the horse, and I couldn't leave him. By the time we got Midnight home, it was late November. The racing season was long over, and the mortgage was due on the ranch. We tried to sell off some of our other horses, but nobody wanted to buy them and feed them over the winter, when they wouldn't be able to use them until spring.

"Allister Gates was in Laramie on business when Frank unloaded Midnight from the train. Allister made an offer to buy the stallion on the spot, but Frank refused to sell him for any price. So Allister found another way."

"I see." Matt Langtry's response was noncommittal, serving as little more than punctuation for the story. Jessie could not see his face, but she was certain his expression would reveal no more than his words. The last thing he'd want would be to feel sympathy for Frank Hammond, she reminded herself. He was only waiting for her to supply him with Frank's alleged motive for killing Allister. Well, fine. He could wait till hell froze over. The coldhearted bully would get no more help from her!

He was taking the mare on a fast climb now, paying scant attention to the trail the horses had left. Above them, the slope ended in a long, rocky ridge that would give them a view of the surrounding hills. With luck, they might be able to see where Frank had gone.

"Let me guess the rest of the story," he said. "Your ranch fell into foreclosure. Allister pulled a few strings, redeemed it from the bank for a song, and claimed the stallion as part of the property."

"But he went too far!" Jessie insisted hotly. "We mortgaged the land and the buildings on it. Allister had no right to the horses, especially the stallion! At the time we signed the loan papers, we didn't even own Midnight!"

Matt exhaled thoughtfully. "I'd have to agree with you there. A good lawyer could have saved you and your brother a lot of grief."

"Lawyers cost money. We didn't have any money. But Frank had every right to take the stallion away. That's what he told Allister. Unfortunately, the man wouldn't listen."

They were approaching the top of the ridge. Maybe she should take care of the marshal now, Jessie thought—get the gun, or grab a rock somehow and knock him out. Then she could take the key and her pistol and be gone before he came to. Frank had to be somewhere close. If she could find him and unlock the handcuffs, he'd be free to ride for the safety of the mountains.

To accomplish that, however, she would have to act fast and decisively. Matt Langtry was a powerful man. Her only hope would be to take him by surprise.

Rimrock, higher than a man's head, jutted like a row of monstrous teeth along the ridgetop. Matt guided the mare through an opening between the stone spires. Jessie was glancing around for a loose rock she could reach and use as a weapon when she felt him stiffen against her.

"Down there," he said softly.

Thoughts of an attack fled from Jessie's mind as

she peered past his shoulder, following the line of his gaze far down the slope.

Two brown horses, Matt's tall chestnut and the bay he'd brought along for Frank, stood side by side on the rim of a deep gully.

Both their saddles were empty.

Please God, no! Jessie leaned forward against him, her hands digging into his sides, as the mare rocketed down the slope. *Please let Frank be all right,* she prayed silently. *If he's hurt, please don't let it be too badly.*

She leaped to the ground as Matt pulled the mare to a halt. Stumbling forward, she passed the horses and reached the lip of the gully ahead of him.

Scoured out of the earth by centuries of spring runoff, the gully was a stone's throw across and more than fifteen feet deep. Its crumbling sides were dangerously steep, its dry bottom scattered with gravel bars, round boulders and clumps of sage. The bleached bones of an animal, most likely a calf or sheep, lay partly buried in mud and sand.

Unable to trust her quivering legs, Jessie dropped to her knees and leaned over the edge. Her eyes searched frantically in both directions, as far up and down the gully as she could see. Maybe Frank wasn't down there. Maybe he'd fallen earlier, and the horses had run on without him, finally stopping here, where they couldn't cross. Maybe he'd crawled out of sight and was hiding somewhere, scratched and bruised but alive.

He had to be alive, had to be safe. Sweet, gentle Frank had never hurt anyone in his life. Surely God wouldn't allow him to come to harm.

She felt a light touch on her shoulder and realized that Matt Langtry had crouched beside her. Silently he pointed to a spot directly below them, half-hidden by the branches of a scraggly juniper. Only then did she see the faded blue of a trouser leg and the dark shape of a boot.

"No!" She flung herself over the edge and onto the slope, sliding and tumbling downward to reach her brother. Scrambling to stay upright, Matt followed her. His boots set off showers of dirt and rocks where they dug into the crumbling bank.

"Stay back, Jessie!" he barked. "Let me get to him!" But she paid him no heed. Her only thought was for Frank, who lay sprawled below her on his back, his manacled arms pinned awkwardly beneath his body. With his hands free, Frank might have been able to break his fall. As it was, he had tumbled helplessly down the steep slope, battering his head and body on every obstacle he passed.

As she clawed her way closer, she could see his face. His eyes were open, staring vacantly into the blinding glare of the sun. A thin trickle of blood had formed and dried at the corner of his mouth.

Even before she touched him, Jessie knew that her brother was dead.

Seconds later, Matt reached the bottom of the slope. He found Jessie cradling Frank in her arms, rocking him like a child. Her black curls had tumbled over her face, hiding her expression, but the keening sobs that rose from her throat told Matt all he needed to know.

He swore silently as he took in Frank's glazed eyes and the unnatural set of his head on his broken neck. This was the last thing he'd wanted to see happen. He had been responsible for the safety of his prisoner, and he had failed in his duty.

Not only that, but after Jessie's account, he'd almost begun to believe that Frank could be innocent. Now the question of his guilt would be nothing but empty debate. Frank was dead—as dead as he would have been at the end of a hangman's rope.

Reaching down, he touched Jessie's shoulder. Through the thin fabric of her shirt, her flesh was taut and quivering. "I'm sorry," he said. "I'll help you get him up to the horses."

"Don't you touch my brother!" She turned on him, spitting out the words. "He's not your prisoner anymore. This is over, no thanks to you, Marshal! Go away and leave us alone!"

Her tear-reddened eyes blazed wounded fury.

Matt knew she blamed him for this tragedy. But if she hadn't held him up at gunpoint and forced him to dismount, he would have remained at Frank's side. With any luck at all, the two of them could have eluded the vigilantes together.

It was Jessie's interference that had caused Frank Hammond to bolt off alone. But this was no time to point that out.

"You can't stay here, Jessie. And neither can Frank, unless you want to leave him for the buzzards and coyotes. We need to get his body back to town."

"No!" The cry exploded from her throat as she clung fiercely to her brother. "I won't have him paraded down Main Street for people to stare at! Frank isn't a convicted criminal. He doesn't belong to you, and I won't let you have him!"

"Your brother was arrested, Jessie. He died as a fugitive." The words came out sounding cruel, but some things had to be said. "We have to follow procedure—"

"Hang your damned procedure! So help me, I'll kill you before I let you take him!"

Matt hesitated, weighing his choices. It wouldn't set well with the sheriff, reporting Frank Hammond's death without bringing in the body. But right now there were more urgent things to consider. Jessie was half out of her mind with grief. Leave her alone, and anything could happen. He had one tragedy on his conscience. He didn't need another.

"All right. We'll do this your way. Tell me what you want."

A look of surprise flashed across her face. Then, as if through an act of will, her features arranged themselves into a calm mask. "I want to take him home," she said. "I want to bury him on the hilltop above the ranch, next to Mama and Papa. That's what Frank would want."

"Then that's what we'll do. I'll tell the sheriff what happened, fill out the paperwork and hope for the best."

She nodded grimly, offering him no thanks. "Get these miserable handcuffs off him. If you hadn't forced him to wear them, Frank would still be alive."

Matt made no reply. It was standard procedure to handcuff a prisoner during a transfer. But Jessie would have no interest in hearing that.

Taking the small key from his pocket, he crouched beside her. Together they turned Frank's body onto its side. For her sake, he worked gently and carefully. Frank was beyond hurting, but he knew Jessie would feel the slightest strain, twist or pinch as if were happening to her own flesh.

When the manacles were removed, Jessie lowered Frank's body to the ground. Then, with her mouth set, her eyes brimming, she stepped back and allowed Matt to lift her brother in his arms.

Frank Hammond had not been heavy in life. His lanky teenaged body, still in the process of growing, was little more than bones and sinew. Matt needed no help carrying him out of the gully, laying him across the saddle of the spare horse and lashing his body into place. It was a shame neither of them had brought a blanket. It might have been easier on Jessie if they'd been able to wrap him.

Anxious to be done with this sad business, he swung onto the back of his chestnut gelding and waited while she mounted her mare. Without a word, she moved in front of him and headed south, keeping below the ridge. Matt savored the glint of sunlight on her raven curls as he rode a few yards behind her. He found himself missing the grip of her hands at his waist and the lightly electric pressure of her breasts against his back.

Jessie would not have an easy time of it, with her brother dead and her ranch gone. With no resource except her beauty, she could easily go the way of too many pretty girls and end up making her living on her back.

By all the fires of hell, Matt vowed, he would shake the life out of her before he'd let her do a thing like that!

His own vehemence startled him. Years ago a retired sheriff, who'd been a friend and mentor, had warned him that getting involved with any woman on a case was a surefire recipe for trouble. Matt had always followed that advice. He would continue to follow it, even now.

Especially now.

Jessie Hammond was the prettiest girl he'd ever seen, and only six or seven years his junior. She was spunky and tender, with a vulnerability that roused all his protective instincts. But he wasn't about to become involved with her. He was only concerned for her welfare. And besides, this wasn't even his damned case!

Or was it?

Once again Matt ran her story through his mind—the ill-fated purchase of the stallion, the foreclosure on the ranch, the seizure of the horse and the fight with Allister Gates. If there was one common thread that ran through Jessie's retelling, it was that Frank had been the one in charge. Frank had mortgaged the ranch. Frank had bought the stallion. And Frank had been the one to go and take the horse back.

That, Matt realized, was what bothered him. He had met both the brother and the sister. Frank had been quiet, almost timid, scarcely capable of violence, let alone murder. The bold one of the pair had been Jessie. Willful and audacious, she might have deferred to her brother as the man of the family, but in a crisis, she would have been the one to act—or at least to push him into action.

Matt stared at her proud, slender back, struggling against the flow of his thoughts. What if both Frank and Jessie had lied to him? What if she'd gone with Frank that night, to cover him with the rifle while he took the stallion? If Allister had tried to stop them, it would have been Jessie who'd stood in his way.

And it would have been Jessie who'd shot him.

Chapter Four

They rode single file over unmarked ground. Jessie led the way on her mare, her rigid shoulders betraying her tightly reined emotions. Matt followed a few yards behind her on his tall chestnut, leading the bay with Frank Hammond's body slung over the saddle. He had hoped Jessie would talk to him, maybe tell him more about what had happened. But she hoarded her secrets as she hoarded her grief, locked in some deep place he could not reach.

Let it go, logic tempted him. With Frank Hammond dead, the murder of Allister Gates should be a closed case. Frank was beyond punishment, and if this dark sprite of a woman had fired the fatal shot, then dropped the rifle in the confusion of getting away, the consequences would haunt her to the end of her days. Surely justice would be served well enough.

The argument made all the sense in the world. But Matt had sworn an oath to uphold the law, and he did not take that oath lightly. He had lost a prisoner entrusted to his care. That meant he no longer had the option of walking away. Whatever the cost, it would be his duty to uncover the truth and to act on that truth.

Even if getting to the truth meant destroying Jessie Hammond.

They were moving deeper into the hills that formed the skirts of the Big Horn Mountains. The aspen groves were giving way to the forests of pine that carpeted the slopes as far as the timberline. Above them, still blanketed in snow, rocky peaks jutted against the sky.

Matt had assumed she was leading him back to her ranch. But no one would build a homestead on this steep, remote landscape. Jessie, he suspected, was taking him someplace else.

"I'm new to these parts," he called out, breaking the long silence. "Which way is your ranch?"

"You mean the place that *used* to be our ranch." Her reply was blade thin, blade sharp. "It's due east of here, in a hollow on the other side of that long ridge. We'll pass the graveyard on the way down. But right now we're taking a side trip. There's something I need to do."

The steely undertone in her voice warned him

against asking her more. As she spoke, she swung the mare left and cut down the hill toward what looked like an overgrown box canyon. Matt followed her, taking care to see that the steep descent didn't cause her brother's body to slip off the horse. Damn, but he'd be glad when this grim errand was done and Frank was planted in the family graveyard where she wanted him.

But even then, the trouble would be far from over. Matt couldn't walk away from this mess now; he was in too deep. Justice demanded that he learn the full truth about Allister's death. For that he would have to win Jessie's trust, even if it meant betraying her later.

They had reached the box canyon he'd seen from above. The mouth was narrow and overgrown, its entrance hidden by a high tangle of oak brush. Inside, stream-fed alders reached almost to the top of the sheer rock walls. Fingers of water from hidden springs trickled over the grassy floor.

Not until the mare nickered, and the gelding began to snort and toss its head, did Matt realize what the canyon held.

Through the trees, he could make out flashes of motion and the glint of sunlight on an ebony coat. Then, as he followed Jessie into the clearing, he heard the challenging scream that only a stallion would make. The sound raised gooseflesh on the back of his neck.

The horse had been hidden in the deepest and narrowest part of the canyon, penned in by a sturdy six-foot log fence. It bugled again as they came closer, stamping its hooves and tossing its elegant head.

Arabians were a small breed as horses go, and this stallion was no exception. But the sheer power of its compact body, the delicacy of its spring steel limbs, the grace of its arched neck, tapered muzzle and high, plumelike tail almost took Matt's breath away. He had always appreciated fine horses. Copper, his own superb chestnut gelding, was his proudest possession. But without a doubt, this fiery stallion was the most magnificent horse he had ever seen.

Nervous as a cat, it snorted and danced away from the fence as they approached. It would take a rare natural gift to bond with such a high-strung animal, Matt thought. Had young Frank Hammond possessed such a gift?

But the answer to that question no longer mattered. Frank's gifts, and whatever might become of them, had ended in tragedy at the bottom of a rocky gulch.

As Jessie swung off her mare and walked up to the gate, the stallion raced away in a burst of speed, its tail flying like a banner, its nostrils drinking wind. This horse had cost the lives of two men, Matt reminded himself. Was it possible that such a beautiful creature could bring tragedy to anyone who possessed it?

Tethering the two geldings at a distance, Matt dismounted and walked toward the fence where Jessie stood. The stallion, which had been approaching her cautiously, snorted and dashed away.

"Virgil Gates is going to want that stallion," he said. "If the papers on the mortgage and the sale are in order, I'd be willing to witness that the horse is legally yours. Then, maybe, you could strike a bargain with Virgil—the stallion for the deed to your ranch. Then, at least, you'd have a roof over your head."

Jessie shook her head vehemently. "I don't do business with the devil. Virgil's not going to get his hands on Midnight. Nobody is."

Her tone was gritty and cold. Caught off guard, Matt stared at her.

Her eyes blazed back at him, steely with determination. "You have something that belongs to me, Marshal. My pistol. I want it back."

"Don't be a fool, Jessie."

"You have no right to order me around. What I do with my own property is none of your business."

"But, for the love of heaven, the horse—"

"My brother's dead because of this horse. So is Allister Gates. Now give me the gun."

Mute with horror, Matt drew the Peacemaker out of his holster. Jessie was acting out of grief and rage, but she was right about one thing. He had no legal right to stop her from shooting her own horse.

She could turn the gun on him as well, he realized. But if he wanted to win her trust, he would have to take that chance.

Keeping the muzzle pointed downward, he offered her the grip. She took the pistol from him and turned away without a word. Stunned, he watched her walk to the gate and unfasten the twisted length of wire that held it closed. Dragging the clumsy structure partway open, she walked into the enclosure. Matt heard the click as she thumbed back the Peacemaker's hammer. He cursed himself for not having had the foresight to remove the bullets.

Planting herself a few paces from the opening, she gave a low whistle. The stallion pricked up its ears, nickered and trotted toward her. Matt held his breath, knowing better than to interfere. If the horse sensed danger, it might rear and crush her with its hooves. But to his amazement, the creature appeared completely trusting. It stopped in front of her and lowered its exquisite head, as if waiting to be stroked.

Now it remained only for Jessie to point the muzzle of the gun at the spot below the stallion's ear and pull the trigger. Her free hand rose and stroked the satiny neck. Matt couldn't see her face from where he stood, but he could see that she was trembling. *Stop!* he wanted to shout at her. *You don't have to do this!* But the words froze in his throat.

Jessie raised the gun, her finger tightening on the

trigger. For a moment time seemed to stop. Then, abruptly, she moved to one side, exposing the open gate. The pistol bellowed as she fired.

Matt heard the stallion scream. Its body hurtled past him, almost knocking him down as it flashed out of the gate. As he reeled sideways, the awareness sank in that Jessie had shot into the air.

Dizzy with relief, he watched the black horse thunder down the canyon and disappear. It would be all right, he told himself. The Big Horn Mountains were vast and deep, dotted with high, grassy meadows where wild mustangs ran free. With luck, the stallion would find a new life there among its own kind, and no one would ever lay a rope around its elegant neck again. But Jessie Hammond had just thrown away the last chance of redeeming her ranch.

Torn between outrage and jubilation, Matt turned back toward Jessie. In freeing the stallion, she had committed an act of reckless audacity—an act of mercy, an act of love. He did not know whether to shake her, hold her, or simply turn his back and walk away.

In the corral, Jessie had crumpled to her knees. Matt reached her in a few strides and bent down to clasp her shoulders. As he lifted her to her feet, the pistol dropped from her limp fingers and fell to the ground.

She sagged against him, her throat jerking. "I couldn't shoot him—" she gasped. "I wanted to. I wanted to kill Midnight for destroying Frank. And I wanted Virgil Gates to find the body. I wanted him to know that he hadn't won." Her hands clenched on Matt's chest. "But I couldn't do it. I looked at Midnight and I—couldn't!"

Matt's arms tightened around her. She was so small and wounded and alone, her vulnerability tore at his heart. His protective instincts surged. He found himself wanting to comfort her, to fight her battles and keep her from harm. Without conscious thought, his lips nibbled along her hairline, tasting the sweetness of her skin. She was as soft and warm as a child.

For a moment her breath seemed to stop. She gave a tremulous sigh and began to melt against him. Then, abruptly, she stiffened in his arms. Bracing her hands against his chest, she shoved him firmly away. Shards of ice glittered in her eyes.

"Maybe I should have shot you instead," she said coldly. "Heaven knows, you're more to blame for Frank's death than that wretched stallion!"

Spinning away from him, she scooped up the gun, checked the hammer and thrust it into the pocket of her baggy overalls. Then, without another word, she stalked to her mare and sprang into the saddle.

For the next half mile she barely stayed in sight. Matt followed the flash of her red plaid shirt through the trees, cursing as he trailed behind with Frank's body. He had taken on the simple errand of bringing in a prisoner, something he'd done without mishap hundreds of times in his career as a lawman. Now he found himself dealing with a dead body, a possible unsolved murder and a woman who was driving him crazy!

Only one thing was certain. If he had the sense of a mule, he would keep his horny hands off Jessie Hammond. She might be as tempting as a fresh plum tart with cream, but her kind of trouble was the last thing he needed—especially if he ended up having to arrest her for the murder of Allister Gates. Feigning friendship to get her to talk was part of his job. But making love to her could be the worst mistake of his life.

He could see her now, paused on the ridge above him, glancing back over her shoulder as she waited for him to catch up. Well, let her wait, Matt thought. He'd had enough of her games. It was time he stopped panting after her like a schoolboy and did his job. He had two deaths to investigate, and Jessie was his only link to the truth. He would get to that truth, he swore, no matter what it cost him.

Jessie watched Matt Langtry as he wound his way up the slope. He moved the horses at a deliberate pace, taking care with Frank's body on the turns. He did not look up at her.

She forced herself to keep still and wait for him, even though her nerves screamed with the urge to race on ahead. To keep running would only make things more awkward between them. Sooner or later she would have to stop and let him catch up. It might as well be now.

Still trembling, she raked her windblown hair back from her face. Her fingertips brushed the spot along her hairline where his lips had nibbled a brief path. The sweetness of that small caress had almost undone her. She had wanted nothing more, at that moment, than to sink into his arms, bury her face against his shirt and cry her heart out.

No one had held her in a comforting way since the death of her parents in a blizzard four years earlier. Frank had been the focus of her love between that time and now, but there had been no outward affection between the two of them. They had been partners in survival—close in spirit, but private and proper in terms of physical affection.

Only when Matt had pulled her against him and brushed that light caress along her hairline did Jessie realize how lost she'd felt and how hungry she was for the strength of a man's arms.

Terrified by the rush of emotion, she had pushed him away and lashed out to protect herself. Matt Langtry's actions had tipped the scales against her brother's life. If he'd manacled Frank's hands in front instead of behind, or if he'd given her the key when she'd demanded it, this tragedy would never have happened.

How could she forgive him for that? How could she let him touch her, when her heart screamed against what he'd done and what he stood for? The law was always on the side of rich landholders like Allister and Virgil Gates. Poor farmers and homesteaders didn't stand a chance.

Holding the mare in check, she waited for Matt to bring the horses up onto the ridge. Her heart crept into her throat as he came closer. It was easy to hate him at a distance. But when he was near she felt confused and vulnerable. It was all she could do to keep from kicking the mare and bolting off at a gallop, just to get away from him.

As he came abreast of her, he cast an impersonal glance in her direction. His face was as expressionless as a granite slab. He had chosen to ignore her, she thought. Fine, that would make everything easier.

Avoiding him with her eyes, she nudged the mare to a brisk walk. He stayed at her side, moving in close enough for conversation. It seemed he wasn't going to make things easy after all. Jessie's heart slammed against her ribs as she waited for him to speak.

"How well did you know the Gates brothers?" It was his lawman's voice, flat and relentless in its demand for answers.

"I hardly knew them at all," she answered truthfully. "I knew who they were, of course. I'd seen them in town and on the road. But I don't recall exchanging a word of polite conversation with either Allister or Virgil. Ranchers and homesteaders don't exactly socialize in these parts."

"Or any other parts that I know of. What about your brother? What kind of dealings did he have with them?"

"None—until last fall when Allister laid eyes on the stallion. As I told you, he made Frank an offer in Laramie, and Frank told him the horse wasn't for sale at any price. That's the last we heard until the week when the Felton marshal served us with notice that the Gates brothers had redeemed our mortgage and we had three days to clear off the property. Later that day, Allister came by with a half-dozen cowhands from his ranch and took the stallion."

Even as she spoke, Jessie was amazed that she could tell the story so calmly. There had been nothing calm about that afternoon. The men from the Gates Ranch had galloped up to the house armed with pistols. They'd caught Frank outside, unarmed except for the heavy double ax he'd been using to break up a stump. Holding him at gunpoint, they'd put a lead on Midnight and taken the stallion out of the corral. Jessie had rushed outside in time to stop her brother from hurling his ax at Allister, which would have surely gotten him shot.

"You have no right to take that horse!" she'd shouted as Allister's men led the stallion down the trail. "He's not part of the ranch. He's ours."

Allister Gates had shot her a contemptuous look, spat in the mud and ridden away.

Frank had been beside himself. It had taken all Jessie's persuasive powers to keep him from getting his rifle and going after Allister Gates right then. But that didn't mean he'd murdered the man. If he had, he would never have been able to keep it from her.

She glanced back over her shoulder to where her brother's body lay slung across the bay horse. Now that Frank was dead it would be all too easy to blame him for killing Allister. Case closed. Frank was beyond judgment, but his name would be forever tainted with the stain of murder. And the real killer, whoever he was, would go unpunished.

Whatever the cost, Jessie vowed, she would not allow that to happen. She owed it to Frank and to their parents' memory to clear his name. And the one man who might be able to help her was riding at her side. No matter how much she might resent him, she could not afford to drive him away.

"What can you tell me about the Gates family?" the marshal asked, breaking the silence. "Did Allister leave a wife? Any children?"

"That's a story in itself," Jessie said. "The Gates brothers were both bachelors, and since Allister was in his fifties and Virgil in his forties, nobody expected that to change. Then, last summer, Allister made a trip to St. Louis and came home with a wife."

Matt gave a low whistle. "You're right. That is a story in itself. What's she like?"

"Younger—a widow, I'd guess. Nice looking. And she knows how to dress. I've seen her in town a few times, but that's all. I can't say I know her."

"Do you know her name?"

"Lillian—I heard someone call her that."

"Lillian." He repeated the name thoughtfully, as if he were tasting each syllable. Maybe the marshal had an eye for rich, good-looking widows, Jessie thought with a stab of irritation.

Impatient, she seized his arm. "Don't you see? Now she owns half the ranch. And Virgil owns the other half. If he marries his brother's pretty widow, he gets it all! Virgil had a lot more motive for killing Allister than poor Frank ever did!"

"So how do you explain the fact that Allister was shot with Frank's gun? Nobody could have known the gun would be there."

"No, but Virgil could have found it and seen the perfect opportunity to kill Allister and let Frank take the blame. Or it could have been someone else— maybe one of the ranch hands who had a grudge against Allister. Heaven knows, he wasn't the most likable man in the world."

"I thought you said you didn't know him."

The coldness in Matt's voice hit Jessie like a slap. For the space of a breath, she weighed the wisdom of telling him about Allister's behavior when he came for the stallion. No, she decided, that would only lend weight to the case against Frank.

"I know him by reputation. From all reports, Allister Gates was an arrogant, abrasive man."

"But I'll wager he wasn't stupid. Allister had to have known the horse wasn't his to take. My guess is, if you'd called his hand, he would have given the two of you a choice—the horse or the family homestead."

"And he was betting we'd choose to give up Midnight rather than lose the ranch. Allister didn't need our land, and neither does Virgil. But now he'll take the place. It's that or lose his money."

Matt exhaled wearily. "You should have kept the stallion, Jessie. With Frank gone, you might have been able to trade with Virgil and keep your home."

Jessie shook her head, fighting tears. "Frank died for that stallion! I won't dishonor his memory by giving up Midnight to Virgil Gates!"

They were coming over the last ridge now. Gazing down into the narrow valley below, Jessie could see the cabin, with its outlying clutter of sheds, corrals and pens that had been her home for the past fifteen years. It was a poor and shabby place—calling it a ranch bordered on a joke. But she'd been happy here. The years of poverty and backbreaking work had been sweetened by the harsh splendor of this mountain country, the warmth of family love and the beauty of horses. Her father had spent some time among the Shoshone and had learned the skill of "Indian breaking" a horse with gentleness and trust. Horses broken by Tom Hammond were valued by cowhands and ranchers all over the county. Even the big roan that Morgan Tolliver favored had come to him by way of the Hammond Ranch.

Tom had passed his horse-breaking skills on to his children. But his unexpected death had left them ill-prepared to handle the business of horse selling. Worse in terms of the future, more blooded horses were being imported from the East and bred on the big ranches. There was less demand for the wild-caught mustangs that had furnished their livelihood for years.

Jessie and her brother had been at the point of selling out when Frank had seized on the idea of buying a prize stallion. Midnight had become his dream, then his obsession. Now there was nothing left.

"Where will you go, Jessie?" Matt Langtry asked her. "Have you made any kind of plans?"

Jessie stared down the hill at the ruin of her world.

"No," she said, swallowing the ache in her throat. "Frank and I were given three days to clear off the property. That time will be up tomorrow night. But I'm not leaving the county. Not until I know who really murdered Allister Gates."

Chapter Five

The Hammond family graveyard lay on a flat knoll above the ranch. Amid the scattered clumps of mallow and blue-eyed grass, Matt could make out five graves. Two of them were adult sized with names and dates carved into crude wooden slabs. The other three were nothing more than weathered, overgrown baby mounds with no markers. Stillborn children, Matt guessed. A woman giving birth could have a bad time in this isolated spot, especially in winter, with no doctor or midwife able to get through the snow.

Would it have been Jessie who attended her mother? He pictured her frightened young eyes in the lamplight, her small hands doing what needed to be done. Swiftly he willed the image away. Life had toughened Jessie Hammond. He admired her strength and courage. But that didn't mean he could afford to sympathize with her, let alone like

her. Until the murder of Allister Gates was resolved, he would have no choice except to view her
as a suspect.

Jessie had left him here and ridden on down to the
ranch to put away her mare and get a shovel. She
had made a point of telling him that the graveyard
was outside the boundary of the homestead. They
wouldn't be burying Frank on property that belonged
to Virgil Gates—or to Lillian Gates, Matt reminded
himself. Now, that was a situation that warranted
some checking into.

Looking off the knoll, he could see Jessie coming
back up the path on foot. She moved with a determined stride, balancing two shovels under her left
arm. In the crook of her other arm she carried a rolled
bundle wrapped in a sheet of oilskin.

Above her, boiling black clouds spilled across the
sky. Sheet lightning danced above the western peaks,
followed by a distant echo of thunder.

"Here." She flung one of the shovels at him. "Unless we want to finish in a storm, we'll need to get
this grave dug in a hurry."

"Fine. Let's get to work." Matt jabbed his shovel
into the sod to mark the edge of the grave. He would
have been willing to do the job by himself—Lord
knows, he'd dug graves alone before. But Jessie was
right about the coming storm and, for all her doll-like
size, she'd proved she was no weakling. Maybe the

effort of digging would release some of the grief and anger she held so tightly in check.

"Do you have any place to stay when you leave the ranch?" he asked her as they scooped away the rocky earth. "Any family? Friends?"

"Are you making me an offer?" She shot him a scathing glare.

"Not unless you want to share a single bed in a boardinghouse." Matt saw color flood her cheeks and couldn't resist adding, "Of course, if we could work it out with my landlady, I'd be happy to accommodate you."

She lowered her blazing face. "Don't be smart with me," she muttered. "I don't need your help, or anybody else's. I can manage just fine by myself."

"Can you?" Matt thrust his shovel into the ground and scooped up the rocky soil. "I've known other pretty women who thought they could manage by themselves. I don't even want to tell you what became of them when their luck ran out and they had no place to go."

"Then don't tell me. I can guess. And it's not going to happen to me. I'm strong and I'm good with horses and cattle. I'll find work."

"If you can find anybody who'll hire a woman, especially the sister of the man arrested for killing Allister Gates."

Her head jerked upward, eyes wide and angry.

For the space of a breath, Matt thought she might swing the shovel at his head. Then her shoulders sagged. "Frank was innocent. I've told you all the reasons why. But you still don't believe me, do you?"

"What I believe doesn't count for much. It's what other people believe that's going to determine how they treat you."

"You're saying I should leave? Make a new start someplace where nobody knows me? Maybe change my name?" The blade of her shovel crunched into the dirt. "I happen to be proud of my name, and I'm not about to see it stained by lies and deceit."

Behind her, lightning flickered across the sky. Thunder growled as the fast-moving storm crept closer. Dirt flew from their shovels as they flung their efforts into finishing the grave ahead of the rain.

The grim line of Jessie's mouth was softened only by the satiny fullness of her lips. She worked intently, stabbing her shovel into the ground with a force driven by pain and fury. Matt had no doubt she meant what she'd said about clearing her brother's name. He'd known plenty of women in his life, but never one who possessed such dogged determination as Jessie Hammond.

One question gnawed at him. If she'd shot Allister why would she be so bent on clearing her brother, especially when it would be easy to let him take the blame? Was she the virtuous young woman she appeared to be? Or did that china-doll face and those melting amethyst eyes hide the heart of a backwood Jezebel who'd do anything—lie, seduce, even kill—to get what she wanted?

He studied her furtively, his attention lingering on a bead of perspiration that had pooled in the hollow of her throat. He found himself wondering what it would be like to lick that bead away, savoring the salty taste of her sweat as he nibbled his way upward to her mouth…or downward to the cleft between those luscious breasts….

Matt jerked himself back to reality. Fantasizing about Jessie might be delicious, but after a while, he knew, it wouldn't be enough. He would want her. And he couldn't have her, not as long as she was a suspect in his murder investigation.

For now, he could only regard her as an intriguing puzzle.

By the time the grave was deep enough, the storm had moved in. Black clouds, split by crackling thunderbolts, seethed overhead. The air was heavy with moisture.

There'd been no time to prepare a coffin. But now Matt saw what Jessie had brought up the hill, bundled in the oilskin sheet.

Placing the bundle on the ground, she unfolded it with careful, tender hands. Inside was a beautifully pieced patchwork quilt. Noticing the lack of wear

around the edges, Matt judged that it must be new—
a treasure in this rough place.

Jessie looked up at him, fighting back tears. "It's
a wedding-ring quilt. My mother made it for the girl
Frank would find and marry one day. But now
there'll be no girl, no marriage, no children. Only
this." She rose to her feet and turned toward the horse
that carried her brother's body. "Help me lay him on
it," she said.

Matt knew better than to protest, even though this
seemed a waste of so much loving work. Frank
would have rested just as well in the oilskin or the
bare earth and never known the difference. But if it
would ease Jessie's heart to wrap him in the quilt
meant for his bride, who was he to argue against it?

With Matt cradling Frank's head and shoulders
while Jessie supported the feet, they eased the lanky
body off the horse and laid it out on the beautiful
quilt. Sensing that she wanted to do the rest alone,
he stepped back and watched as she crossed his
hands over his chest and tucked the quilt around him.
When everything but his face was covered, she bent
and kissed his waxen forehead. "Sleep tight," she
whispered, as she must have done countless times
when her brother was small. Then she folded the
quilt over his face and rose to her feet.

As she did so, raindrops spattered around them,
drenching their hair and clothes. Hurrying now, they

used the oilskin to lift the body and lower it into the grave. Then Matt reached down and pulled the waterproof ends over the quilt.

"Go on," he said. "Take the bay down to the house and get dry. I can finish up here."

Water streamed off her hair, beading on her ebony brows and lashes as she shook her head. "We can't just leave," she argued. "Not without saying words over him."

Matt sighed. This was the part of burials he always dreaded most. And standing here in the rain didn't make things any pleasanter. "Go ahead," he muttered. "Say whatever you need to, but make it fast."

"You first."

Matt bit back a growl of protest. Meeting Frank Hammond had set loose a whole string of calamities, and the last thing he felt like was finding something good to say about the poor young fool. But Jessie was waiting, so he clasped his hands, bowed his head and fumbled for some words that wouldn't add to her anguish.

"Lord, only you know what was in this boy's heart, and only you can be his judge. We ask you to see the good in him and to welcome him home. Amen."

She shot him a startled glance, and he realized he should have said more. But never mind. He was done, and now it was her turn. He might as well let her talk as long as she wanted. They were already soaked to the skin and couldn't get any wetter. He watched her in silence as she stared down at the bundle in the open grave.

"I know people will say you've gone to a better place, Frank," she began. "But you were in a good place right here, and you left it too soon. You missed the chance to finish growing up, to get married, to have children, and to grow old on this earth. And you left with people accusing you of something I know you didn't do."

She paused, swallowed and licked a tear from her lips. "It's too late to undo the wrong and bring you back. But I'm not going to let it rest, Frank. Whatever it takes, I'm going to bring Allister's killer to justice and clear your name. I swear it on your grave, and on Mama and Papa's graves." She drew in an anguished breath, like the sound of tearing silk. "That's all I have to say, I guess. Except that I love you. I didn't say it much when you were alive—I mostly just scolded and bossed you. But I'm saying it now, just in case you're someplace where you can hear…"

Her voice trailed off as she turned away and picked up the shovel where she'd left it thrust in the ground. Dirt and rocks spattered on the wet oilskin as the first scoop of earth dropped into the grave.

Matt followed her example, digging deep and hard into damp soil and flinging it down into the hole. He wanted to be done with this sad business and get out of the rain. Better yet, he wanted to wake up in his own bed and realize that he'd dreamed this entire hellish day and had never known Frank or Jessie Hammond.

Jessie worked beside him in silence, her hair hanging over her face in curly black strings. Her soaked flannel shirt clung beneath the baggy overalls, giving him glimpses of her voluptuously curved little body. Matt tore his eyes away. This was a funeral, not a damned peep show, he reminded himself. He'd be smart to keep his eyes, and his thoughts where they belonged.

After the grave was filled and smoothed over, they mounted in the drizzling rain and rode down the hill. Matt was spattered with mud from head to toe and so cold that his teeth were chattering. He knew that Jessie must be the same. Yet she sat like a queen in the saddle, head erect, spine ramrod straight, ignoring her own misery. She was a proud thing. Too proud, he thought. With no family, no home and no money, she was going to need help. The sooner she accepted that fact, the better off she would be.

When he got back to Sheridan, he would make some inquiries. Maybe there was a family who needed an extra pair of hands, or better yet, a hotel or boardinghouse where she could work for room, meals and a little spending money. It was a servant's job she'd be doing, but that couldn't be helped. Since no rancher would hire a woman wrangler, let alone the sister of Frank Hammond, there wasn't much left to choose from except the saloons and dance halls. And he would lock her up in jail, by heaven, before he'd see men touching her the way they touched girls in those places.

Touching her…the way he was aching to touch her now.

By the time they arrived at the ranch, the rain had turned the yard to a quagmire. Leaving Matt to put the horses in the shed, Jessie hurried to the house to make a fire and start some coffee.

Crossing the porch, she paused to kick off her muddy boots, as she'd always done. Only then did it strike her that it made no difference whether she left muddy tracks across the floor or not. Tomorrow the place would no longer be hers.

Since the boots were off by then, however, she left them on the porch and pattered inside. She would need to get out of her wet clothes, but first she'd start a fire in the big cast-iron stove that warmed the house. Thank goodness Frank had filled the wood box two days ago. At least there'd be plenty of dry kindling.

The truth struck like a sudden blow, choking her with tears. Traces of Frank were all around her—the neatly chopped wood, the clothes in his room, the razor and shaving brush on the washstand, the book left open on the table. She almost expected to glance out the window and see him come whistling around the corner of the house. But no, she had to accept the fact that he was gone. She would not see him again in this life.

She jammed the kindling into the stove and added a few scraps of carefully hoarded newspaper. The blaze flickered and caught the dry wood. When it was burning well, she closed the grate, measured coffee and water into the big tin pot and set it on to boil.

The air in her bedroom was icy, but with Matt around the place, she could hardly risk leaving the door open to warm the room while she changed. Her teeth chattered as she stripped off her sodden clothes. Beneath them, her skin was puckered with gooseflesh. Her nipples were so taut and hard that they ached.

If he were to walk in on her, would he like what he saw? Would he like touching her? Would she like being touched? Jessie blotted the shocking ideas from her mind. What was the matter with her? How could she be having such feelings about the man who'd let her brother die?

As she reached for a clean flannel shirt, she heard the opening creak of the front door. Her pulse broke into a gallop as she heard Matt's voice.

"Jessie?" The door closed behind him. "Are you all right?"

"Just ch-changing." Jessie threw on the shirt without taking time to find a camisole. Her cold-numbed fingers fumbled with the buttons.

"Can I do anything to help?" His deep voice came from just outside her door. "Out here, I mean."

"Just make sure the f-fire hasn't gone out." She shoved her legs into her denims, tucked in her shirttails and yanked the belt tight around her narrow waist. "Coffee's brewing, but it'll be a few minutes yet."

"Fire looks fine, and the coffee's starting to smell good." His voice came from the kitchen now. Since she hadn't heard his footsteps, she could only surmise he'd taken off his boots on the porch, as she had.

"Hope you don't mind if I dry my shirt." She heard the sound of a chair sliding across the floor, toward the stove.

"That's fine." She blotted her dripping hair with a towel and finger-combed the tangles out of it. When wet, her hair became impossibly curly, but that couldn't be helped. Besides, this cocky young lawman, who likely had half the girls in the county chasing after him, wouldn't care how she looked. To him she was only the sister of a murder suspect and a thorn in his side to boot.

She stepped out of the bedroom to find him standing with his back to the stove. His rain-soaked shirt and vest hung over the back of the chair, steaming lightly in the heat. From his lean hips upward, his torso was bare. Jessie forced herself to avert her gaze, but not before catching full view of his broad shoulders and tapering, muscular back. In the firelight, his skin was pale gold, marred here and there by white scars that hinted at the dangerous life he'd lived. His light brown hair clung to his head in flat, wet curls.

Heaven help her, he was sinfully, heart-stoppingly beautiful. And she was guilty of ogling him, but only for the barest moment. Her face flooded with color as he turned around to find her staring at the floor.

"You've…changed your clothes," he murmured, his eyes taking her measure from head to toe. She became aware that the flannel shirt she'd donned so hastily was one that had long since grown too small. Worse, her cold-numbed fingers had missed a button, leaving a gap in the most embarrassing place, and she was wearing no camisole underneath.

Mortified, she spun away from him. Her hands shook as she worked the stubborn button into its hole. The worn fabric strained, pulling tight over her breasts and casting her puckered nipples into stark relief. She fought against the urge to rush back into her bedroom and fling on a different shirt. That would only call attention to the problem, making her look as foolish and flustered as she felt.

Summoning her last shred of dignity, she turned around, just in time to catch a fleeting smile on his face. It was a smile to flutter pulses and break hearts, enhanced by the dimple in his left cheek and the coppery twinkle in his eyes. But Jessie was in no mood to be charmed.

"You must be cold," she said politely. "I have a few old shirts of my father's. You can borrow one while yours dries. Frank's clothes would be too small for you."

Her voice broke as she realized how easily she'd spoken her brother's name, as if Frank had just stepped outside to get some firewood or go to the privy and would reappear at any moment. It would take time to get used to the idea that he was gone— the last of her family.

She was truly alone now. The enormity of that realization made her feel as if she'd tumbled into a vast, black pit and was spinning through space with no hand she could clasp to break her fall.

She willed back a surge of scalding tears. But the tremors that racked her body, like an earthquake rooted in the pit of her stomach, could not be stopped so easily. Her breath came in small, dry hiccups as she fought for self-control.

"Jessie—" Matt Langtry's face was a blur above her, his voice faint and distant. "It's all right, girl. Holding back will only make things worse."

Jessie shook her head, unable to release the dark force that pounded inside her like a helpless fist on a locked door. She wanted to cry—no, to scream, to wail and rant like a madwoman over the injustice of what had happened. She wanted to double her hands into fists and pound the man standing before her. She wanted to bruise his flesh purple, to make him feel the pain she was feeling in every nerve of her body.

She managed one glancing blow to his chest before he caught her wrist and jerked her against him.

"Stop it, Jessie." His arms went around her, pulling her hard against his bare chest. His embrace was not loving or even tender. It was nothing more than an effort to bring her under control. But as soon as she felt his strong clasp, Jessie realized how much she needed to be held. As she sank against him, the spasms subsided to shivers. She gulped in air, filling her lungs as her taut diaphragm relaxed. A single tear squeezed out of her eye, wetting his cool skin.

To the touch, his body was like sculpted hardwood, smoothed to a satiny sheen. He smelled of clean sweat and strong lye soap, and the crisp dusting of hair on his chest tickled her cheek. His hands rested on her shoulder blades, holding her lightly but firmly. Matt Langtry cared nothing for her, and she hated him for his part in Frank's death. But right now he was strength, comfort and protection—everything she needed. She huddled against him, seeking refuge.

"It's all right," he murmured, patting her awkwardly. "Go ahead and cry, Jessie. You'll feel better for it."

But it wasn't all right, she knew. And she would not allow herself to feel better until she had cleared Frank's name and righted the horrible wrong done to her family.

Matt's body was beginning to warm against her. It was time she pulled away, Jessie thought. But she had no will to leave the comforting circle of his arms. His fingers had begun to move, kneading her shoulder blades with a sensitive skill that awakened a moan in her throat. To stifle it, she pressed her face against his chest. His smoky male aroma swam into her senses, making her feel tingly and light-headed. Driven by an impulse she could neither understand nor explain, she extended her tongue and flicked it over his skin. The taste of him was salty-sweet and so intoxicating that she could not resist wanting more. He groaned at her touch and pressed her closer against him—so close that she could feel the hard, bulging ridge of his arousal against her belly. Jessie swallowed a gasp. She had never been this close to a man before or realized she had the power to bring him to such a state. Lord help her, he felt as big as a stallion!

Heat-driven panic shot through her body. Oh, this was wrong in every possible way. How could she be having these feelings when he'd dealt her such a devastating blow? She had to stop this madness—now!

Before she could summon the will to move, he shifted his hands to her shoulders and thrust her away from him. She stumbled backward, her face burning.

"I—think I'll be all right now," she stammered.

His face was impassive, his gaze flinty. "Yes, I believe you will," he said in his lawman's voice. "I'll take that spare shirt now, if it's not too much trouble."

"Yes, I'll get it—and then I'll warm up some venison stew for us." She spun away and fled into her own room, where her father's clothes lay washed and folded in an old wooden chest. She'd put them away for Frank, thinking they might fit when his spindly frame filled out. But now there was nothing to do except get rid of them.

Tomorrow she would bundle up these clothes, along with Frank's, and take them to the Hawkins family who lived in the next hollow. Their three strapping boys would put them to good use. She would take the old milk cow and the four good laying hens as well. She could hardly expect Virgil Gates to care for the poor creatures. As for the horses, they would fare well enough running free in the mountains. She would keep only Frank's sturdy pinto and her fleet-footed mare.

But where would she go? How would she live?

She would be leaving here with no family, no

home and no money. The few neighbors who might take her in were as poor as she was, and she dared not risk putting them in danger from people like Virgil Gates and his vigilantes. Ranchers in these parts would jump at any excuse to attack squatters and drive them off their land.

There was one place where she knew she could find shelter. But it would provide little more than a leaky roof over her head. She would be utterly alone there, and the living would be hard.

Never mind, Jessie told herself as she chose a soft flannel shirt of a brown-and-gold plaid that matched the color of Matt Langtry's eyes. She would deal with tomorrow's problems tomorrow. Right now, the only person who might be able to help her was waiting in the kitchen; and she had just made such a fool of herself that he probably couldn't wait to leave.

Her knees turned to jelly as she remembered the warmth of his arms around her, the smell and taste of his skin and that long, solid ridge that had jutted against her belly, sending ripples of liquid heat through her body. The sensation had transfixed her, melting her will to move.

But the marshal, at least, had kept his head. Thank heaven he'd pushed her away. But what did he think of her now? That she was an easy mark who'd offer herself to any man who seemed interested? That she was out to seduce him into helping her clear her brother? Or did he see her for what she was—a flustered young woman, too inexperienced to know when she'd gone too far?

It made no difference, Jessie told herself. No matter what had happened between them, she'd be a fool to let Matt Langtry walk out of her life. He was the one man who had a vested interest in finding Allister Gates's real murderer.

Or did he?

She had almost reached the bedroom door when the truth struck her with sickening force. Matt would be bound to answer for the loss of a prisoner in his custody. The incident would go on his record, and there would likely be other consequences as well.

For the death of a murderer, he would probably get no worse than a hand slap.

But for the death of a young man who would have been proved innocent…

Jessie's legs quivered beneath her as she walked back into the kitchen. A bright, ambitious lawman like Matt would do almost anything to avoid such a blot on his career. She could not count on him to help her.

She could not count on anyone but herself.

Chapter Six

The top of the crude pine table was worn to a sheen from years of scrubbing. There were no napkins, and the unmatched china dishes were chipped and cracked. But as Matt drank the biting hot coffee and tasted the savory venison stew, he sensed that people had been happy in this little cabin. There had been parents, children, books, animals, laughter and love—all the things he'd missed in his own growing-up years.

Outside, rain battered the sturdy log walls. Water drummed on the windows and streamed over the edges of the overhanging roof. Since there would be no question of his leaving until the storm ended, Matt resolved to take his time, enjoying the warmth of the cabin while he tried to pry more information from his reluctant hostess.

The weather was so black that Jessie had been

forced to light the lamp that hung above the table. The golden light glistened on her damp curls and heightened the porcelain contours of her face. Her eyes were downcast, and a baggy flannel shirt now covered the one he'd seen earlier. The seductive creature with the gaping buttons and tantalizing tongue was nowhere to be seen.

Matt could not deny that he missed her.

He watched as she took small bites of the stew and crusty brown bread as if forcing herself to eat. She'd been through a hellish day, he reminded himself. Under the circumstances, she appeared to be doing all right. But Matt had seen enough grief to know better.

He remembered how she'd trembled in his arms, like a small volcano about to explode. He had meant only to support and comfort her, but the flick of that little cat tongue against his skin had affected him like the touch of flame to spilled gunpowder. The heat had flashed through his veins, igniting a blaze of need in his loins. In an instant he'd been rock hard and aching for her.

Lord, she must have known what she was doing to him. No woman who bred horses could be too naive to know when a man was aroused. So why was she sitting at the far end of the table, buttoned up and glowing like an angel in some old church painting? Blast it, he had a job to do, and Jessie Hammond was driving him to distraction.

Was that what she'd wanted, even planned? What

was going on in that beautiful head of hers? Was she out to win him, divert him or destroy him?

He was damned well going to find out.

"Good stew," he said, breaking off a piece of bread to sop the gravy from the bowl. "Am I right in assuming you made it?"

She looked up, her eyes reflecting glints of golden lamplight. "Yes. After I shot the deer, skinned it out and cut up the meat. I'm not what you'd call a helpless woman, Marshal."

"Call me Matt. And, believe me, helpless is one thing I'd never call you, lady. Especially after the way you shot that Stetson off my head. I take it you've done most of the hunting around here."

"Frank had a soft heart. He never liked killing things. Neither do I, for that matter, but sometimes it's necessary."

"Was killing Allister necessary?"

Her soft lips parted. Then, as the question sank home, her face went white with shock.

"You think *I* killed him?"

"I'm only asking a question. It's part of my job," Matt answered quietly.

She rose to her feet, her hands clutching the edge of the table. "One question doesn't exactly cover it," she retorted. "Did I hate Allister enough to kill him? Absolutely! Am I sorry he's dead? Aside from the consequences to my poor brother, no, not a whit! He was as treacherous as a rattlesnake! The world's a better place without him!"

"So, did you kill him, Jessie?"

Her shoulders sagged slightly. "No. I swear by all that's holy, I didn't kill Allister, and neither did Frank." Her head went up, eyes suddenly blazing. "We had nothing to gain by killing him. After the trouble over the stallion, even a fool would know that one of us would be blamed. As for the rifle—"

"That gun makes for some damning evidence," Matt interrupted her.

"So why in heaven's name would we leave it behind?"

"Panic." Matt studied her, leaning back in his chair. He'd gotten to her, all right. She was like a cornered wildcat, eyes flashing, body poised for attack or flight. "Let say, after you learned the rifle had been lost, you sent Frank on ahead with the stallion and went back for it alone. Allister caught you in the corral, one thing led to another, and the gun went off. When you realized you'd just killed a man, you were so shocked that you dropped it and ran."

She straightened, glaring at him like a teacher about to dress down a backward student. "You know as well as I do that Allister was shot in the back. Whoever pulled the trigger knew exactly what they were doing. And they left the rifle because they wanted it to be found. Now, are we finished with this silly conversation?"

"For now, maybe you should have been a lawyer, Miss Jessie Hammond. You've presented a right smart case for yourself."

"I've done nothing more than point out the truth," she retorted icily. "I know when I'm being tested."

Backing off for the present, Matt glanced toward the counter. "I don't suppose I could trouble you for a piece of that apple pie, could I?"

The glare dissolved into outrage. "Why, you shameless, no-account rascal! First you practically accuse me of murder, and then you expect dessert! I know your kind. I'll bet your mother must have spoiled you rotten!"

"I'm afraid she never had the chance."

"Well, I'm not feeling charitable. For your information, I'd rather throw that pie to the chickens than feed one bite of it to you!" She was putting on a brave front but Matt knew she was crumbling inside. Get her to relax and talk, and he might have some chance of getting to the bottom of this mess.

"All right, name your price. I'll do anything within reason for a piece of that pie—plow the garden, say, or mend that sagging gate on the corral—after the rain stops, of course. You'll have my word on that."

"Mend the gate? Plow the garden?" She flung the words back at him, her voice husky with strain. "I have to leave this place tomorrow! Why should I do anything for Virgil Gates? For that matter, why should I even wash the dishes? I can't take them with me."

"In that case, it would be a real shame to leave that pie for Virgil." Matt fixed her with an appealing gaze.

"You're right." Turning toward the counter, she picked up the tin pie plate. The drumming of the rain filled the silence as she held it between her hands, staring down at the flaky, golden crust and the place where two wedges of pie had been cut and removed.

Suspecting she was about to fling the pie in his face, Matt readied himself to duck. At last, however, she placed it on the table and sank back onto her chair. Her stricken eyes pierced him to the heart.

"I made this pie as a treat for Frank. We each had a piece for supper the night we went after the stallion. I suppose it's a mercy we can't see into the future." She blinked back tears, her voice on the verge of breaking.

"Jessie, I'm sorry—"

"No," she said, cutting off his apology. "Life has to go on, and pies were made for eating." She picked up her knife, cut a generous wedge and lifted it onto a clean saucer. "This is for you, but only on one condition."

"Name it."

"You said your mother never had a chance to spoil you. I'm guessing you had a tough time growing up down Texas way. I'd like to hear a little about it."

Matt let out a deep breath, wishing she'd asked him almost anything else. "It's not a pretty story," he said.

"That doesn't matter." She pushed the saucer across the table toward him. "I just need something to take my mind off all that's happened today."

"In that case, I can tell some very entertaining lies. Wouldn't you rather hear those?"

She shook her head. A smile flickered at the corners of her rosebud mouth, but her eyes were pools of melancholy. "I'd rather hear the truth, even if it isn't pretty."

"Truth is seldom pretty. At least not the truth that I've seen."

"What a cynical soul you are, Matt Langtry." She cut a two-finger width of pie for herself. "What happened to your mother?"

Matt steeled himself against the memory. Strange, how razor sharp it was, even after so many years. "I was seven years old. School was out, and I came to find her at the hotel where she worked. She saw me coming and stepped out into the street…and into the crossfire of a drunken gunfight. She died before she hit the ground."

"You saw it?" Jessie's voice was a horrified whisper.

Matt nodded. "She was all the family I had. All I've ever had."

"What about your father?" Jessie's fork lay untouched next to the saucer of pie.

"I never knew him. I was born on the wrong side of the blanket, as it's so delicately put. Whenever I asked my mother about him, all she'd say was that he was a fine man, and that she'd tell me more when I was older. She never got the chance."

"So you don't even know his name?"

"It wouldn't make any difference if I did. She never told me much, but I've always assumed he had a wife and children someplace else. A lot of men came to Texas to buy cattle in those days, and they tended to be lonely after the long ride."

"You've never tried to find your father or his family?"

"No," Matt lied, denying the forces that drew him like a magnet to the Tollivers. "Even if I knew who they were, why would they want to know me? I could ruin lives just by writing a letter or showing up on their doorstep."

So why, then, had he gone to so much trouble to investigate the Tollivers? Matt asked himself as he cut a forkful of Jessie's pie and chewed it thoughtfully. Why had he spent hours poring through county records and old newspaper editions? Why had he gone so far as to hire a private investigator—a retired Pinkerton agent working out of Laramie—to look into the history of the family? Although he'd hired him two months ago, he had yet to hear anything from the ex-Pinkerton man, a distinguished, gray-haired gentleman named Hamilton Crawford. But in the meantime, Matt had unearthed the fact that Jacob Tolliver had purchased a thousand head of Texas longhorns and driven them north nine months before Sally Langtry gave birth to a son. It didn't prove a thing, Matt knew. But if Jacob Tolliver wasn't his father, then it had to be one hell of a coincidence.

"After my mother died nobody wanted to take me in, so I was sent to an orphanage," he said, thinking of that grim, gray place where laughter was considered a sin. "When I was sixteen I ran away and joined the Texas Rangers—I was a big boy, and I lied about my age. A few months later, they found out how young I was and booted me out. By then I'd learned to ride and shoot. I drifted for a few years before I found work as a town deputy in Winslow, Arizona. After that, it was Silver City, New Mexico, Dutchman's Creek, Colorado, and now Wyoming. Who knows where I'll end up next?"

Matt took another forkful of pie. He'd never been one to talk about himself, but he'd just told this little chit his whole life story. What was the matter with him tonight? He felt as if he'd drunk too much whiskey, even though there wasn't a jug in the place.

"Haven't you ever wanted to put down roots?" Her stunning eyes focused on him over the rim of her coffee cup. "Surely you must have had a few sweethearts here and there."

"A few." More than a few, Matt thought. He liked the ladies and they tended to like him. But he'd never found one who could keep him from moving on. Oh, he'd known some lovely, willing girls. He couldn't fault them. But how did a man make a home when he had no heritage to build on? Without the example of a father, how did a man learn the love, caring and sacrifice it took to be the head of a family? It didn't seem right, asking a woman to share his life when he knew so little about his own beginnings.

In all the years of his wandering, Matt had never found a place where he belonged or a woman who made him feel as if he'd finally come home.

"Right tasty pie," he said, scooping up the last forkful. "I'd say I earned it. For whatever it's worth, you now know more about Matthew T. Langtry than anyone in the county."

Her soft lips smiled at him, contrasting sharply with her tragic eyes. Was she the innocent child-woman she appeared to be? Or did those bewitching features mask the wiles of an accomplished actress, capable of lies, treachery and even murder?

The case she'd made for her innocence had sounded convincing. For a while he'd almost bought it. But her logic, he realized, had been too well thought out, the facts too carefully rehearsed. The picture she'd painted for him was too perfect to be true.

Matt knew better than to trust a pretty face, and

Jessie Hammond's beauty would put a wild rose to shame. All his danger alarms were clanging. He'd be a fool to ignore them.

"Turnabout's fair play," he said, rising from his chair. "I'll help you clean up while you tell me about your own family."

"Not much to tell." She began to gather up the dishes and move them to the pan on the counter. "My father's folks settled Kentucky with Daniel Boone and moved on west when things got too crowded there. My mother was straight from Killarney. She sang the loveliest Irish songs—I've been told I look a lot like her. But she wasn't strong like me. She was always sick with the babies. Most of them she lost. Frank and I were the only ones who…lived."

Matt heard the catch in her voice, and for a moment he thought she was going to cry, but she tightened her lips, lifted her chin and continued. "She and Papa were good people, and they loved each other. They died four years ago when their wagon went off the road in a blizzard. We found them with their arms around each other. I wanted to bury them that way, but Reverend Smith said it wouldn't be fitting. So we laid them out in separate coffins. You saw their graves on the hill."

"You may not think so now, but you were lucky," Matt said. "I can't imagine anything better than growing up surrounded by so much love."

"Yes." She lowered her eyes, soaped a cracked bowl and placed it in a pan of rinse water. "And now it's all gone. I'm as much alone as you are."

The long silence was broken only by the sound of battering rain. Darkness had closed in, and the storm's fury showed no signs of letting up. Unless he wanted to ride down the mountain in a downpour and spend the night on a rock-hard bunk in the Felton jail, Matt realized, he would be stuck here until morning.

There were worse things by far than spending the night alone with a beautiful woman, even a woman he couldn't allow himself to touch. But the situation was going to be awkward. Glancing at Jessie's pensive face, Matt guessed that she must be thinking the same thing.

"If you wouldn't mind lending me a spare blanket, I'd be happy to spend the night in the hay shed," he offered, feigning a gallantry he did not feel.

"The hay shed leaks. And I chased a nest of skunks out of there two days ago. The storm's likely driven them back inside."

"So what would one more skunk matter? That's what you're thinking, isn't it?" Matt kept his face expressionless as he spoke but made no effort to hide the twinkle in his eye.

For an instant she looked startled. Then her mouth twitched into a tentative smile that was like the sun coming out. "Don't be silly. You can sleep in Frank's—" The smile vanished as she corrected herself. "In the room that was Frank's. By morning the storm will be gone and your clothes will be dry. And I can promise you coffee and leftover pie for breakfast."

"Thank you," Matt said, meaning it. "I'd like to repay the favor by checking in Sheridan for someplace where you could live and work—a respectable place, like a boardinghouse or one of the better hotels, or maybe a home with a family."

She shook her head. "Don't trouble yourself. I'd feel trapped in a big town like Sheridan. And I'm not much for taking orders either. Knowing me, I'd end up arguing back and getting myself fired."

"That's pride talking, Jessie. You're going to need some help getting back on your feet. The sooner you learn to accept that, the better off you'll be."

Her jaw clenched stubbornly as she shook her head again. "I can take care of myself," she said. "It's not your job or anyone else's to look after me."

"But where will you go? How will you live?"

"That's my own business." Turning away from him, she wrung out the dishcloth and began wiping off the table.

"That's where you're wrong." Matt took a deep breath, knowing what he had to say next would likely upset her. "There'll be an inquest into your brother's death, and another into Allister's murder. You're a material witness in both cases. You'll need to stay where the sheriff's office can get in touch with you."

Her head shot up, eyes blazing. "Are you telling me that I'm a prisoner?"

"Of course not. But if you leave the county it's liable to get you in trouble."

She carried the dishpan to the door, stepped onto the porch and threw the dirty water out into the rain. When she came back inside, she was shivering. "I'm not leaving. You heard me promise Frank I'd track down the real murderer. That's what I plan to do."

Matt sank onto a chair, feeling weary of the whole miserable day. "Not on your own, you're not. Leave it to the law, Jessie."

The dishpan clattered onto the counter as she spun around to face him. "The law doesn't care!" she snapped. "Why should they care? Why should *you* care? You've got poor Frank to hang the blame on. He's all you need!"

Matt rose slowly to his full height. He didn't often lose his temper, but this irritating person had just crossed the line. As he glared down into her defiant gentian eyes, he could feel himself seething inside. When he spoke, however, his tone was glacial.

"What you're accusing me of doesn't even have a name, lady. I do my job. That means I don't walk away until I've found the truth. If your brother murdered Allister Gates, he's already paid for it. But I promise you on my life, I won't leave it there. I won't give up until the real killer is found and punished."

"Even if you think it could be me?" She spoke boldly, with none of the helpless, fluttery tactics he might have expected from a woman.

"Yes," he answered. "Even if I think it could be you."

For the space of a heartbeat they stared at each other like two enemies meeting on a narrow mountain trail with no room to pass. Then, realizing that more words would only add to the tension between them, Matt stepped away from her and walked toward the bedroom.

"It's been a long day, and I'll be turning in," he said, pausing in the doorway. "I'm much obliged for the meal and the bed. Tomorrow morning after breakfast I plan to ride into Felton and report Frank's…accident. Then I'll see what I can find out at the Gates Ranch. When I'm finished I'll be back to tell you what I learned. You're to wait for me right here, Jessie. I know you need to leave, but don't go without me. Understand?"

After a long hesitation, she nodded and turned away. Matt crossed the threshold and closed the door quietly behind him.

Jessie stood where he had left her, willing herself not to tremble. The lawman's cold determination had shaken her to the core. She'd told him the truth about what had happened on the night of Allister Gates's death. But why should he believe her? The evidence against her was almost as strong as the evidence against Frank.

She'd shown Matt Langtry that she was a crack shot, capable of threatening, if not violent, behavior. He had ample reason to believe that she'd sent Frank ahead with the stallion, then ridden back and shot Allister herself. Maybe he even thought she had something against Frank and had left the rifle to frame him.

What had she done?

The clean bowls rattled in her hands as she stacked them on the shelf. Why bother? she thought. Tomorrow the place would no longer be hers. She might as well fling all the dishes against the wall and break them into a million pieces.

But she knew she would not. Her mother had handled those poor chipped bowls with loving care, knowing there'd be no money to replace them if they broke. Even in despair, Jessie could not bring herself to harm them.

This little ranch and the people who'd called it home had been her world. Now that world was gone. She seemed to be suspended in a void with nothing under her feet or within the reach of her hands. For that brief moment in Matt Langtry's arms she'd felt safe. But that safety had been an illusion. The tall deputy, with his ironclad rules and granite heart, could turn out to be the gravest danger of all.

Wiping her hands on the dish towel, she cast a lingering gaze around the cabin. As she blew out the lamp, she could feel her world crumbling in the darkness. Frank was gone, really and truly gone. He would not be there when she woke up tomorrow. She would never make him another cup of coffee, cut him another slice of pie or wash his dirty overalls. She would never laugh at his silly jokes or hear his tuneless whistle as he milked the cow. He'd been cut down senselessly, stupidly, still in his teens, with his life barely lived.

Frank had been innocent. Yet, he'd been treated like a dangerous criminal, his wrists cruelly manacled behind his back. If Matt Langtry had allowed him to guide his own horse, Frank wouldn't have died. He would be free in the mountains, not lying cold and dead in that sad little graveyard on the knoll.

Tears of grief and rage welled up inside her as she stripped off her clothes and yanked her flannel nightgown over her head. A lot of things had gone wrong today. But fate had hinged on that one small issue. Frank had died because of the handcuffs—and Matt Langtry had locked them around his wrists.

What was done couldn't be undone. But Jessie knew she would never forget—or forgive—what had happened today.

By the time she reached the bed, her legs were shaking. Her throat felt so tight and swollen that she could scarcely breathe. She crawled between the sheets and pulled the covers over her head, trying to shut out the memory of Frank's young body sprawled in the bottom of the wash. But the nightmare was inside her and she knew it would never go away.

She had lost everything.

Chapter Seven

Matt opened his eyes to find her leaning over him. Her face was moon-pale in the darkness, her eyes like luminous violets with centers so large and black that he felt as if he might tumble into them and spend the rest of his life falling.

His throat stirred as he tried to speak, but she laid a cool finger across his lips. Her palm brushed his unshaven cheek. "Shh," she whispered. "Lie still."

As she moved closer, her damp curls skimmed his bare chest. The contact puckered his nipples and triggered a swelling ache in his loins. She smelled of rain and wildflowers and fresh-cut hay. He inhaled her hungrily, filling his nostrils, his lungs and his blood with her essence. He wanted to make her part of him. Heaven save him, he wanted even more to be a part of her, to thrust deep inside her sweet body and feel the ripping explosion of her response.

Cupping the back of her head, he pulled her down to him and tasted her mouth. Her kiss was soft and warm and damp, with lips that opened like the petals of a dark red rose. Her fiery little tongue darted into his mouth, probing delicately, almost timidly. For a long moment he forced himself to remain still while she explored. At last, unable to stand the wait, he answered with his own tongue, thrusting deep and hard, filling her mouth with the way he wanted to fill her body.

He felt her breath stop for an instant. Then she responded. Her tongue went deep. Searing currents jolted through him like chain lightning. The heat of his desire melted away all caution, all resistance. Nothing mattered except having her.

They ended the kiss, both of them breathing hard. Catching her hand, he pressed his lips to her palm, then moved it downward to his swollen erection. Her breath stopped as her fingers closed around him. He gasped, almost bursting at her touch. "I need you, Jessie," he muttered, straining against her. "I need you now."

"And I need you..." She rose above him, wearing a shiftlike gown, so sheer he could see the dark mauve buds of her nipples through the fabric. Her fingers trembled where they touched his swollen flesh.

As he reached up to unfasten the pearl button clasp, the gown parted and fell away from her. Her naked body was exquisitely curved, tapering from the ripe globes of her breasts to her tiny waist to full, fertile woman's hips. His touch between her legs roused a moan of ecstasy. She was slippery wet, eager and ready. "Yes…" she whispered. "Oh, yes, my love…"

Lifting her in his arms he eased her down onto his aching shaft. She uttered a whispered cry as he penetrated her, then sighed with pleasure and began to move with him, matching his thrusts, her body cradling his in tight, silken warmth, her strokes growing more urgent, more frantic…

Damn! Matt jerked himself awake. He lay alone in Frank Hammond's bed, damp and spent and cursing. Outside, the storm drummed on the glass windowpanes. A tree branch scraped against the roof.

The dream had seemed so real that he could still taste her mouth and smell the clean, grassy aroma of her hair. Only now did he realize how much he'd wanted it to be real. But that was crazy thinking, he reminded himself. He was already going to answer for losing Frank Hammond. Bedding Hammond's sister could land him in enough trouble to ruin his career.

But she'd gotten to him today; there was no denying that. And like it or not, he was becoming involved—more deeply involved than he'd ever planned.

Rolling onto his back, he lay staring upward, listening to the rain. He imagined Jessie lying on the narrow bed in the next room, her dark hair spilling across the muslin pillow. He could only hope she was getting some sleep. She'd been on the point of collapse tonight, and he'd been rough on her. After some of the things he'd told her, she would likely hate him. But that was all to the good, considering how badly he wanted to get his hands on her.

Tomorrow morning, rain or no rain, he would remove himself from temptation. At first light he would mount up, ride down the mountain to wire a report of Frank's death to the sheriff. Then, once he found out what had happened to the vigilantes, it would be time to pay a call on Virgil Gates—and on Allister's widow, Lillian.

His musings were interrupted by a low sound that came through the thin plank wall, very near his head. He held his breath, ears straining in the darkness. At first he could hear only the breathy moan of the wind and the pelting of rain on the shingles overhead. Then he heard the sound again. This time he recognized it as muffled sobbing.

Matt sat up and flung back the quilt. He was swinging his feet to the floor when reason caught up with him.

Leave her alone, he cautioned himself. Jessie was grieving, as she had every reason to grieve. If she'd wanted his comfort and advice, she would have asked for it.

Wide-awake, he lay back onto the pillow with his arm beneath his head. He could hear her plainly now.

Her racking sobs went on and on, as if her heart and soul had dissolved into tears that would flow out of her, leaving nothing of Jessie Hammond but an empty shell.

With a sigh, Matt sat up again and reached for his trousers. Jessie was proud, he reminded himself. Judging from the sound of her, she needed a kindly touch and a listening ear. But she would never ask for comfort, especially from him. As for his offering it—Matt shook his head. Reaching out to comfort Jessie would be like trying to soothe a wounded wild-cat. All the same, he felt obliged to try. He was all she had.

Standing up, he buttoned his trousers over the long cotton underwear he'd worn to bed. Then, still barefoot, he opened the door and stepped out into the cold kitchen.

Jessie's door was closed, but there was no lock on it. When she failed to answer after several light raps, he spoke.

"Jessie, are you all right?"

Ear to the door, he waited for her reply, expecting her to order him crossly away. But he heard nothing. Even the sound of her furious weeping had stopped.

"Jessie?"

There was no answer.

Cautiously he cracked open the door. In the dark room he could make out her small form, curled like a baby beneath the quilt. Her shoulders quivered. Her breathing was muffled and jerky.

Leave her alone, Matt cautioned himself. Sooner or later she would cry herself out and fall asleep. Tomorrow she'd be stronger, ready to face whatever came next. Jessie Hammond was a tough woman. She would be all right.

But what if she wasn't? Doubt gnawed at him as he willed himself to close the door, as he considered all she'd lost.

Matt sighed. If anything happened to Jessie because he'd walked away when she needed help, he knew he would never forgive himself. But he was facing his own risks. Once he set foot inside that bedroom, he'd be walking a tightrope. One misstep and he'd be up to his ears in trouble. He couldn't afford to let that happen.

Steeling his resolve, he opened the door again. The worn plank floor creaked under his bare feet as he walked to the bed. Jessie had not moved. She lay in a ball, her hair spilling from beneath the quilt. Matt cleared his throat and spoke softly.

"Are you all right, Jessie? I'm here if you need to talk."

She did not respond, but he could hear her ragged breathing. If she was pretending to be asleep, it wasn't much of a performance.

"Jessie?" He touched her shoulder through the

quilt. A shudder passed through her tautly quivering body, but she did not answer him.

Moving slowly and carefully, he took the edge of the quilt and eased it down to uncover her head and shoulders. "It's all right to grieve, girl," he murmured. "You don't have to hide your—"

"Frank's dead!" She flew at him in the darkness, her hair wild, her fists pummeling his chest, arms and shoulders. "My brother is dead, and it's—your—fault!"

"Jessie—" He struggled to grip her flailing arms. "Frank's death was a tragedy, but I didn't—"

Her fist caught his jaw in a knuckle punch that made his vision blur. "You handcuffed him! A nineteen-year-old boy who'd never hurt a soul. And you wouldn't give me the key. I keep imagining him, trying to stay on the horse with no hands, clinging with his legs, so scared, so helpless. And I see him pitching into the gulch, with no hands to stop him…no hands…"

Her breath came in wrenching gasps as she vented her fury. Her fists drummed his chest as if she were trying to pound the words into his heart.

Seizing her shoulders, Matt thrust her away from him. "Stop it, Jessie," he growled, bracing her at arm's length. "I know you're grieving, but hurting me won't take away the pain. Your brother's death wasn't my fault. I was only doing my job. And it wasn't your fault. You were only trying to save him. If anyone's to blame, it's the person who shot Allister."

She gazed up at him with tear-swollen eyes. "But it would have been such a little thing for you to leave his hands free. Frank would never have tried to get away. He was too scared for that."

Matt recalled the shy, gangly boy who'd ridden out of Felton with him that morning. Jessie was right, he admitted grudgingly. There'd been no need for him to cuff Frank Hammond. He'd simply followed procedure without giving it a second thought. Then everything had gone wrong.

Hellfire, what a mess!

Jessie was sagging against his grip now, her rage spent. In her simple white nightgown, she looked like a little girl who'd awakened crying from a bad dream. He found himself aching to rock her in his arms and tangle his fingers in her soft, damp curls.

He released her. She swayed unsteadily, then sank against his chest with a weary sob. Matt hesitated, battling his own resolve. Then his arms went around her. Tomorrow she might hate him, but right now she needed to be held, and he was the only comfort at hand.

Crying softly, she trembled in his arms. Lord, but it felt good, holding her like this. Too good, Matt thought. But he could no more let her go than he could will himself to stop breathing. Her hair smelled like rain and sweet grass, the way it had in his dream. He brushed it with his lips, lightly, so that she wouldn't feel it and pull away. Her curls were soft and damp against his skin.

He held her carefully with his hands discreetly placed on her shoulder blades. Even so, the feel of her naked skin through the thin flannel nightgown seemed to sear his palms. It was all he could do to keep his hands from moving lower. The imp stirred and jutted like a flagpole, straining at his trousers as he imagined cupping her firm little buttocks and pulling her in hard against him. Matt eased himself away from her, cursing his own weakness.

"You'll be all right, Jessie," he murmured, hoping talk would distract her from his condition. "You'll hurt for a while, but you're a strong woman. You'll find the courage to go on."

"Will I?" She jerked away, her eyes blazing up at him. "How do you know that? Can you see into the future?"

"No. But I've seen your courage. You can do anything you put your mind to."

"Anything?" She mocked him furiously. "Can I pull money out of thin air and save my home? Can I track down Allister's killer and march him to the gallows? Can I bring my poor, innocent brother back to…life?"

Her voice broke and her chin began to tremble. "You don't know anything about me, Marshal, and you don't care. As long as you can make yourself believe I'll be all right, you can walk away and file your damned report with a clear conscience. Frank Hammond died escaping justice. His sister will get along fine. Case closed." Her hand went up as the last words exploded out of her. *"Damn you and all lawmen to hell!"*

Her palm smacked resoundingly across Matt's face, stinging him to fury. His hands seized her arms, yanking her against him with her face inches from his own.

"Watch it, lady. You can only push me so far, and we're just about there!"

She made an angry sound. Her bare foot came down on his toe. Pain shot up his leg.

All in all, it seemed like as good a time as any to kiss her.

His mouth came down hard and hungry on hers. His arms yanked her close, crushing her breasts against his chest. For an instant she fought him, pushing and squirming. Then the last thread of resistance seemed to break in her. She went molten against him, her arms catching his neck, her frantic fingers furrowing his hair.

Matt's own caution evaporated in the heat of her response. He was on fire for her. His arms molded her to him, kneading her back, pressing her hips against his bursting shaft. "Damn it, Jessie," he muttered against her lips, "you're burning me alive. If you don't stop me—"

She blocked his words with her mouth, her tongue

thrusting, jousting with his. His frantic hands fumbled for the hem of her nightgown and worked their way beneath it, finding her satiny thighs. With his last shred of willpower he bypassed the nest of curls that lay at their apex and let his hand move up to the sweet ripeness of her breasts. She gasped at his touch, arching against his palm as he cupped her sweet, warm flesh. The feel of her was pure, hot need.

But it was the wrong kind of need, Matt reminded himself. Jessie was a bundle of raw emotion—grief, anger and pain. What she was feeling now had nothing to do with desire, let alone love. She was frantic for relief, nothing more. If he took advantage of her now, she would hate him forever.

But how much would she hate him if he thrust her aside and walked away?

Taking a deep breath, he eased his hands from beneath her nightgown. His arms gathered her close, holding her gently. "I want you so much it hurts, Jessie," he whispered against her hair. "But not like this, with you in so much pain that you can't know your own mind."

She clung to him, not answering. He could feel the tension in her, feel her desperate need for relief, and he knew that words wouldn't be enough to ease her.

"Lie down, Jessie," he whispered, guiding her back onto the bed. "I won't hurt you."

He pressed her back onto the pillow. Her eyes

were wide in the darkness, her mouth moist and swollen. Her breath came in tiny, audible gasps.

"Lie still," he whispered. "You'll be all right."

Softly he kissed her lips, her cheeks, her eyelids, tasting the salt of her tears. Her hands clutched him desperately, working his shoulders like the paws of a needy little cat. A whimper quivered deep in her throat.

"Tell me if you want me to stop." He kissed her again, his hand sliding beneath the hem of her nightgown. Gently his fingers stroked their way up her inner thigh. Her breath caught, then her legs parted to open the way for him. The temptation to pull down his trousers and vent his own urgency was there, but Matt willed it away. If he hurt her he would never forgive himself.

She gasped as his fingers found her moisture-slicked folds and the small nub that lay like a pearl at their center. With a little cry, she exploded against his hand, once, then again and again, straining upward until there was nothing left.

Utterly spent, she sank back against the pillow. Burning with tenderness, Matt tucked the quilt around her. Then he bent and kissed her forehead. "Don't even think about this, Jessie," he said. "Close your eyes. Get some sleep. You'll feel better in the morning."

Her breath eased out in a long sigh as she snuggled into her nest of covers. By the time Matt had reached the door of her room and closed it behind him, she was already settling into sleep.

Jessie awoke to the squawk of a magpie outside her bedroom window. Her eyes shot open, then squinted shut, dazzled by the glare of sunlight. What time was it? How long had she slept?

Still groggy, she sat up and rubbed her eyes. Little by little the gray weight of memory crept over her. Yesterday Frank's death had been like a fresh cut, sharp and shocking. Today it had sunk deeper to become a sick, black hollow in her soul. This, she sensed, was how she would feel for a long time to come.

The aroma of hot coffee wafted through the cracks between the planking. For a fleeting instant she thought of Frank. Then she remembered that Matt Langtry had spent the night here. And then she remembered everything else.

Her face went hot as the memory flashed over her—his arms, his mouth, his gentle, expert fingers touching her in places no man had ever touched her before. And her own fevered response—Lord, she'd flung herself at him, panting and moaning like a strumpet!

How could she face him this morning after what she'd let him do? What in heaven's name could she say to him?

Mortified, she pulled her legs against her chest and buried her face against her knees. From outside her window she could hear the scolding magpie. *Shame! Shame! Shame!* the bird seemed to be saying. Jessie had always seen herself as a good woman, like her mother. But she'd thrown that away last night, in the arms of a man she scarcely knew.

And the worst thing was, she'd liked it.

A sweet-hot quiver passed through her body as she remembered how his kiss had captured her, shattering her fragile defenses, and turned her into a wanton beggar. She'd needed that kiss, that seeking tongue, those hands on her body. And she'd needed the blessed, explosive release that his skilled fingers had given her.

He could have taken her, she realized. And in her desperate state of mind she might have let him. But Matthew T. Langtry had been in perfect control. He had wisely and kindly spared her maidenhood.

So why did she have this sudden urge to strip him naked, coat him with honey and stake him out on an anthill?

Maybe it was because even when he was making love to her, the marshal had remained mindful of his duty.

"Shame! Shame!" The magpie squawked and flashed away, reminding her that it was time to get up and begin what was bound to be a miserable day.

Her first task would be to take the cow and chickens, along with Frank's clothes, down the canyon to the Hawkins family. On her return she would turn the spare horses loose to run with their own wild kind. That done, she would deal with the heartbreaking job of clearing her belongings out of the house and choosing what to carry away with her.

On top of all that, she would have to face Matt Langtry and find some way to recover her dignity.

Setting her jaw, she pulled on her shirt and denims, found clean stockings in the chest and shoved her feet into her work boots. A glance in the watery mirror confirmed that she looked awful—no surprise there. Her eyes were red holes in her blotchy face, her hair a tangled mess. But what did it matter? Where she was going today, there'd be no one to care how she looked.

All the same, she took a moment to splash her face, rinse her mouth and run a brush over the surface of her hair. If Matt was waiting for her out there in the kitchen, she needed to face him looking confident and strong.

She would show him…

Squaring her shoulders, Jessie walked to the closed door and put her hand on the latch. It would be easy, she told herself. All she had to do was thank him politely for his help, show him to the door and bid him a firm goodbye. She could manage on her own now. She would have to.

The door swung open. Jessie stepped into the kitchen, expecting to see Matt at the table smiling his cocky, know-it-all smile.

No one was there.

The coffee he'd made was simmering on the back of the stove, and his clothes were gone from the chair where he'd hung them to dry. A glance into the room where he'd slept showed the bed neatly made, with her father's flannel shirt folded on the coverlet. But Matt was nowhere to be seen.

Vaguely uneasy, she walked out onto the porch. The storm had passed, leaving a sunlit spring day in its wake. Chickadees flitted in the aspens and a mourning dove called from the top of a pine. Water vapor curled from the steaming rooftops.

The horses milled in the corral, munching the hay that had been put down for them. Jessie could see her own mare among the green-broke mustangs, along with the pinto that Frank had favored. But two horses were missing. One was the bay that had carried Frank's body back to the ranch. The other was Matt's chestnut gelding.

Jessie's heart dropped as she saw the fresh hoofprints in the mud, leading down toward the wagon road. She should be glad Matt Langtry was gone, she told herself. Now she could get her day started without having to face him.

But the weight in the pit of her stomach was too

cold and bitter to be denied. Matt had not wanted to see her this morning. He had left without even saying goodbye, and after the way he'd behaved he probably wouldn't be coming back.

Chapter Eight

As he rode down the trail, Matt willed himself not to look back over his shoulder. He knew there would be nothing to see. Jessie would be mad as spit to find him gone. She'd likely be hurt as well. But she was far too proud to come galloping after him.

It was better this way, he told himself. Their searing encounter in the night had left him shaken. Facing her this morning, especially if she chose to talk about it, would only make things more awkward between them.

Not that this was goodbye. In a few hours he would need to go back and find her, as he'd promised.

The trail down the canyon was steep and muddy. Matt gave Copper his head, knowing the big chestnut would find the surest footing on his own. The morning was fresh and sunny, the air alive with the songs of celebrating birds.

Above the canyon, two ravens swooped and soared in a wild mating display. As he watched, they flew upward until their bodies were nothing but black specks against the sun. Then, clasping each other's talons, they tumbled downward, over and over in an ecstatic spiral. Just as it appeared they were about to crash into the ground, they separated and flapped upward to perform the whole giddy ritual again. Matt had never thought he would envy birds, but it struck him as a thrilling way to make love.

He groaned inwardly as his thoughts returned to last night. Jessie had been beautiful and tempting and needy. Any thought that she might have planned to seduce him was banished by the memory of her flying fists. She had been in real distress; he was certain of that. But what about him? What had driven him to seize her in his arms, kiss her until he ached and use his touch to carry her over the brink?

Matt had been in and out of more romantic entanglements than he cared to remember. All he'd ever needed to do, it seemed, was smile and wink at a likely lass, whisper a few flatteries in her ear, and she'd be his for as long as the fun lasted. But there was one ironclad rule he'd made and never broken— he always left his ladies as pure as he found them.

But Jessie Hammond defied every rule Matt had ever made. All his instincts told him that her searing innocence was real. But the sensuality she exuded was enough to make his blood boil. Last night, when she'd caught fire in his arms, he'd felt himself burning with her, consumed by her heat. Only the fact that he'd climaxed earlier, in the dream, had saved him from tumbling over the brink of control. Even now, the memory made him want her so much it almost made his teeth ache. The fact that he mustn't have her only heightened his desire.

The ravens had climbed to the peak of the sky once more. Turning his eyes away from their dizzying descent, Matt rode on.

By the time he reached Felton it was midmorning. Matt found Marshal Heber Sims dozing on a bunk in the empty jail and decided to let the old man sleep. The telegraph office was vacant as well. A note on the locked door explained that a tree had blown over on the line in last night's storm, and the telegraph would be down until further notice.

With mixed feelings about the reprieve, Matt led the bay horse down the street to the livery stable. At least he'd have time to do some investigating before he reported Frank Hammond's death to Sheriff Canton.

No matter what he might learn, Matt knew that the death of a prisoner would be a blot on his spotless record as well as on his own conscience. If Frank turned out to be innocent, that blot would be even darker. But it was the truth that really mattered, he reminded himself. And if the truth could ease Jessie's heart, that was the most important thing of all.

At the livery stable, he left the bay and asked directions to the Gates Ranch. The two workmen tending the horses glanced uneasily at each other when they noticed the star on his vest. Matt would have bet good money that they'd ridden with the vigilantes. But when they politely pointed him on his way, he decided not to raise the question. Most lynch mobs were a mix of bad apples and decent citizens. For now, he would give these two the benefit of the doubt.

The turnoff to the Gates Ranch lay three miles south of town on a well-traveled road. On approach, the two-story ranch house looked to be in the midst of a remodeling job. Scaffolding rose above the entrance where a grand-looking portico with columns was going up to cover the modest front porch. Iron grillwork had been added to the plain windows on the first floor, and shutters on the second. The sounds of hammering rang on the clear morning air. So much activity struck Matt as odd, in view of the family's recent loss. But the project had clearly been started weeks ago. It made sense that Allister's widow would want the place presentable for the visitors that would come by after tomorrow's funeral.

Matt tied his horse to the hitching rail. Ducking hammers, he mounted the front steps and raised the lion-headed knocker on the freshly painted door.

The man who answered was middle-aged with a dignified black face. His formal dress and painfully stilted manner proclaimed him to be a trained butler, likely brought from St. Louis by the new Mrs. Gates. A butler on a Wyoming ranch. What next? Matt wondered as he followed the man into a lavishly appointed parlor. Clearly, Allister's widow appreciated the finer things in life.

"Mister Virgil's out back tendin' to a foal," he said in response to Matt's inquiry. "But Miz Lillian's upstairs. I'll go tell her you're here, Marshal."

"Fine, I'll wait."

Matt shifted uneasily, aware that his boots were leaving mud on the cream-and-gold Persian carpet. Whoever had decorated the parlor had decent, if expensive, tastes. The walls were covered in cream paper with pale gold stripes. The apple-green draperies on the tall windows matched the velvet pouf that sat in the center of the floor. The settee and matching chairs were covered in dark brown velvet and decorated with small gold cushions. A gleaming sideboard held crystal goblets and a decanter of what appeared to be brandy.

Matt was gazing up at the glittering chandelier when the subtle creak of a floorboard galvanized his nerves. Reflexively he spun around, hand flying to his pistol grip. But the figure who stood in the doorway was not a gunman but a woman.

She was dressed in a subdued black gown, which did nothing to dim the effect of her voluptuous figure and upswept red-gold hair. The tracery of fine lines beneath her eyes showed her to be in her mid thirties but detracted little from her stunning features—the moss-green eyes, the pouting lips and the small heart-shaped mole on her cheek.

Lillian Gates was, indeed, a woman to kill for.

Taking charge, Matt walked toward her. "I don't believe we've met, Mrs. Gates," he said. "U.S. Deputy Marshal Matthew Langtry, at your service. My condolences for your loss."

Jessie guided her mare up the steep trail from the Hawkins cabin. The sunlit day and cheerful birdsong mocked the gloom that had settled over her spirit.

Grant and Mariah Hawkins had been grateful for the cow and chickens and the bundle of clothes she'd brought them. They'd offered her shelter, as Jessie had known they would. But the last thing she wanted was to bring trouble down on an innocent family. She had thanked them and assured them that she'd be fine on her own.

Now all the work that remained was to free the mustangs, pack what she could carry on Frank's pinto and head up the mountain to the old trapper's cabin in the summer pasture. The cabin would need a lot of work. The sod roof leaked, the wind whistled between the logs and a plague of vermin nested in every dark corner. But the whole summer lay ahead. She would have plenty of time to make the place secure and warm before winter set in.

As for other needs, there was a stream nearby with good water. Roots and berries grew in the meadows and the hunting was good. Jessie knew she wouldn't starve. But she would be completely alone for the first time in her life. The thought of that aloneness was the most fearful thing she had ever faced.

But she wouldn't be alone all the time, she reminded herself. There would be occasional trips into town for news and supplies. And there was the promise she'd made to clear her brother's name. Keeping that promise would mean watching, listening and asking questions. For that she would need to be in town, or even at the Gates Ranch.

For now, only one thing was certain. She had a lot of careful planning to do.

She was turning the mare toward home when a movement on the trail below caught her eye. For an instant her heart took wing. Then, as she realized what she was seeing, Jessie's stomach clenched.

A band of riders—she counted six—had appeared around the bend in the wagon road. They were headed straight for the trail that climbed the slope to her ranch. It was easy enough to guess who they were. She'd been told she had until sundown to clear out, but Virgil Gates had sent his thugs out early to look over the property.

How long would it take them to reach the ranch? Twenty or thirty minutes, she calculated. Less if they picked up speed. She had planned on having time to pack her things and say goodbye to her home. But she should have known Virgil wouldn't play fair.

Spurring the mare, she dashed up the trail. It made sense that Virgil would want to see the property left in good condition. But Jessie knew the kind of men he would send on such an errand. She'd seen his hired guns in town and even knew some of their names. Two of them, especially, made her flesh crawl. Lem, square-built, pugnacious and filthy, had a missing front tooth. Tall, whip-lean Ringo, who wore black and spoke in elegant phrases, had a zig-zag knife scar down his face, and eyes as cold as a rattlesnake's.

Those violent brutes would be capable of looting, rape, even murder if Virgil were to unleash them and turn his back. But even at the risk of having them corner her, she would not allow Virgil Gates to possess what he had no right to take.

Flying into the yard, she swung the corral gate open wide. As the mustangs streamed past her, bound for the freedom of the hills, she caught Frank's docile pinto and tied it to the fence while she got the packsaddle. Her mind was already ticking off a list of what was most important to take—guns, bullets and tools first, then bedding, clothes and food. She would grab as much as the horse could carry, bundle it into a quilt and lash it to the saddle with ropes. There'd be time to rearrange it for better balance after she got away.

By the time the pinto was loaded, Jessie was drenched in nervous perspiration. From down the trail she could hear the snort of approaching horses. Minutes from now the riders would be here. If they caught her, anything could happen.

But there was one thing left for her to do. Something she owed her family. Something she owed Frank.

The cabin and sheds were rain-soaked on the outside. But their inner walls and contents were dry. Seizing a jug of kerosene, Jessie splashed most of it inside the cabin. What was left went on the hay and the buildings in the yard. Even the privy was doused.

With the horses tied at a safe distance, she struck three of the matches she'd crammed into her pockets. Choking on fumes and tears, she tossed them through the open door of the cabin. The kerosene flamed up with an explosive hiss. By the time she reached the hay shed she could see fire dancing behind the glass panes.

It took only one match to turn the hay into a torch. The burst of heat was so sudden that it singed her hair. Through the billowing smoke, Jessie could see the riders coming up over the lip of the trail. There were shouts and curses. Had they seen her?

There was no time to set fire to the other structures, but the sparks from the burning hay would likely do that job for her. Jessie plunged through the smoke and vaulted onto the back of her mare. Dragging the loaded packhorse by its lead, she charged up the hill toward the trees.

"I loved my husband, Marshal." Lillian Gates dabbed at her eyes with a lace handkerchief. "Allister was good to me. I'm the last person on earth who'd want him dead. Surely you're not accusing me of—"

"Not at all," Matt assured her. "I only want to hear what happened the night of your husband's death, everything you saw and heard."

"Oh, must I speak of it? It's so very painful for me…" Fresh tears welled in Lillian's stunning eyes. If she wasn't grieving she was a damned good actress, Matt thought.

"It's important," he said. "I need your help to make sure justice is done."

"But they've caught that wretched boy! It's all settled, isn't it?"

"Nothing's settled until the verdict's read. Meanwhile, it's my job to find out exactly what happened."

"Oh…very well." Her restless fingers twisted her gold wedding band. "I've relived that night again and again," she said with a catch in her voice. "It's my fault as much as anyone's, you know. If I'd insisted that Allister wake up some of the men, he'd still be alive."

Matt shifted on the velvet settee, leaning toward her. "Don't blame yourself. Just tell me what happened, starting with Allister's redeeming the Hammond ranch and sending his men to claim the stallion."

"Why, Marshal!" Her hands fluttered theatrically. "I was Allister's wife, not his business partner. He didn't discuss the affairs of the ranch with me."

"But he'd wanted the stallion for a long time. Frank Hammond told me—"

"Don't you dare mention that murderer's name in my house!" she hissed.

Matt nodded, refusing to be distracted. "All right, then, I learned that your husband made an offer on the horse months ago, in Laramie."

"There's no law against offering to buy a horse." Lillian leaned back in her chair and regarded him with heavy-lidded eyes. "And if Allister claimed the stallion later, it was only because he'd redeemed the Hammond property, and as part of that property, the horse was rightfully his. My husband was not a thief, Marshal."

"Did he have enemies? Anyone who might want to harm him?"

"No!" Her eyes misted, and she stifled a sob. "Allister was the soul of kindness! He didn't have an enemy in the world except for the miserable coward who shot him in the back!"

Matt frowned. "I have to ask you this. Who stands to profit from your husband's death?"

Her hand went to her throat. "Why, no one, Marshal! Allister's share of the ranch will pass to me, of course, but as his wife, it was already as good as mine. And Virgil's share will remain the same as always. Surely you don't think—" The color rose in her face. "My husband was killed in a fight over a horse! A fool horse! I wish to God that he'd just let the wretched animal be stolen! It wasn't worth his life!"

Or Frank Hammond's life, Matt thought. "Tell me what you remember about that night. How did Allister know there was someone in the barn?"

"My husband and I had stayed up late playing cards. We'd just gone to bed when we heard the horses fussing around. Allister pulled on his clothes, grabbed his pistol and ran outside to see what the commotion was about."

"You say Allister took his gun. Did he use it?"

Lillian's pearl earrings quivered as she shook her head. "He may have used it to threaten the thief. But I only heard one shot—the one that killed him!"

She buried her face in her hands, her shoulders

shaking. When she looked up at Matt again, her face was dewy with tears. "When I heard the gun go off, I threw on my dressing gown, lit a lantern and ran outside. Someone was galloping down the drive, but it was too dark for me to see who it was."

"What about the hired hands?"

"They were asleep in the bunkhouse. The gunshot woke them, but by the time they got outside, I'd already found Allister. He was lying facedown in the corral…" Her breath sucked in painfully. "His pistol was on the ground, a few steps away. It hadn't been fired."

"And the rifle?"

"One of the men found it a few paces from his body." Her fingers twisted the wedding ring. So far her story matched what Matt had already heard. It was the discrepancies that always sparked his interest. So far he'd heard none.

"How long had your husband been gone when you heard the shot?"

"Not very long. I remember lying there, wondering if I should get up and light a lamp or just wait for him to come back to bed. Then I heard the gun go off."

"And how long was that? Five minutes? Ten?"

She hesitated. "Somewhere in between, perhaps. Why, is it important?"

"Maybe." In Jessie's version of the story, they hadn't heard the gunshot at all. The time would have to have been long enough for Frank to get back across the river and for the two of them to ride out of hearing range. One of the two women was either mistaken or lying. And one key player in the story was still unaccounted for.

"Where was Virgil while all this was going on?" he asked her.

"I can answer that question, Marshal." The bull-necked man who strode through the doorway seemed to crowd the room. After seeing him ride past at the head of a mob, Matt would have known Virgil Gates anywhere; but this was his first chance to study the man's features. What he saw was a fleshy, handsome face, the wide mouth crowned by a thick wheaten mustache. Horse-sized white teeth flashed when he spoke. His eyes were the color of a frozen lake.

"I went into town around eight for a few drinks and some poker," he said affably. "I was at Smitty's Saloon till around eleven—you can take my word, or you can ask the old man who tends bar. By the time I got home, my brother was dead."

"You didn't hear anything? Didn't see anybody on the road?"

Virgil raked his sweaty blond hair back from his forehead. His skin was pale above the hat line, the mark of a man who'd spent his life outdoors. "Not a soul. But would you take the main road back to town if you'd just stole a horse and shot a decent man in the back?" He glanced around as if looking for a place to spit. "I hope the judge hangs that back-shooting little bastard high and slow, and I plan to be there to watch every minute of it."

"I've heard rumors that you and your friends were out do the job yourselves," Matt said.

Virgil looked startled for an instant. Then he grinned. "Hell, Marshal, me and the boys were just out for a little ride. No law against that, is there?"

"Not if you didn't kill anybody, there isn't," Matt said. "You and your friends were lucky."

Virgil's eyes narrowed. "So what brings you out this way, Marshal? I thought you had the murderer locked up in the county jail."

"Just checking evidence, making sure we know what happened," Matt replied. Sooner or later, he knew, word would get out that Frank Hammond was dead. But until he'd filed his official report, the secret would remain his and Jessie's.

The thought of Jessie filled Matt with a sudden sense of urgency. He'd ridden off and left her this morning, telling himself it would be less painful for them both. But what if he'd been wrong? What if she'd needed him and he hadn't been there for her?

Jessie was an independent woman, but she was alone and vulnerable. It was time he finished up here. He would take a few more minutes to talk with Virgil and to interview the butler and the ranch hands.

Then he'd mount up and ride for the mountains. The sooner he got back to her the better.

"Have they set a date for the trial?" Virgil asked. "We'll want to be there, of course. And I'm guessing you'll need Lillian for a witness."

"Oh, must I go?" Lillian's pained eyes darted from one man to the other, as if seeking a rescuer. "All the terrible memories of that night—I don't think I could stand reliving them."

Virgil gazed down at his brother's widow. In his eyes, Matt glimpsed something he'd failed to notice until now—a glimmer of protective, possessive heat. Heaven help him, the poor brute was in love with her!

Virgil rested one ham-sized hand on Lillian's shoulder. "Don't worry about it," he said. "I'll be there for you. You'll be fine, Lil. Just fine."

Chapter Nine

By the time Matt got back to town, angry clouds
were spilling over the peaks of the Big Horns, threatening an afternoon storm. The mountain trail would
be slippery in the rain. But he'd been in worse places,
and it would take more than a little mud to keep him
from getting back to Jessie.

What he'd learned about Allister's death from the
servants and ranch hands had scarcely been worth his
time. The few cowboys who weren't out on the range
had claimed to be asleep when the fatal shot was
fired. None of them had witnessed anything of im-
portance. And they'd sworn that Frank Hammond
was Allister's only enemy. If anyone but Jessie was
to be believed, the man had been a candidate for
sainthood.

As for Virgil, he would have been at the top of
Matt's suspect list, but the aging bartender at Smitty's

had confirmed his alibi. Virgil had been playing poker until eleven. Then he'd left, presumably for home and presumably alone.

Before leaving town, Matt paid a quick call on the undertaker, who had Allister's body laid out in a costly walnut casket for tomorrow's funeral. The murdered man, ten years older than his brother, looked weary, almost elderly, lying there in his black suit and starched white shirt, with his thin gray hair carefully combed over his pink scalp. His only visible injury was a curved, purplish bruise on his temple—the kind of mark that would be left by the hoof of a shod horse.

"Take a good look, Marshal," the undertaker said. "This time tomorrow, he'll be in the ground."

"Thanks, I've seen enough." Matt took note of the funeral time. If he could rustle up some clean clothes, he might want to pay his respects. A lawman could learn a lot at funerals just by watching and listening. But what mattered right now was getting back to Jessie.

Thunder boomed across the sky as he left the main road and headed up the mountain. Ignoring spatters of rain, he nudged the gelding to a trot. Higher up, the going would be slow and treacherous. The more trail he could put behind him before the storm got worse, the better.

Jessie's face filled his thoughts—the flash of her

heart-stopping violet eyes, the softly swollen lips that he had kissed…and kissed…

But what was he thinking? Jessie had every reason to hate him. She'd be more likely to meet him with a rifle aimed at his chest than with open arms. And he'd promised himself he wouldn't touch her again. Break that promise, and he might as well turn in his badge. As long as Jessie was a suspect in Allister's murder, he had to keep her at arm's length.

Most of her story rang true. The only discrepancy lay in when that shot was fired. Lillian had claimed to have heard it minutes after her husband left the house. Jessie had insisted she'd heard nothing, which would mean that she and Frank were out of earshot, riding for the hills, when Allister was killed.

So who was he to believe? A woman who had just gained half-interest in a ranch, or a woman who, at the time of the murder, had been helping her brother steal a horse from the victim's property? The hoofprint on Allister's head supported Jessie's story. But it did not refute Lillian's. Allister could have been struck by the horse at any time during the struggle.

By the time Matt reached the place where the trail cut upward from the wagon road, the rain was coming down in gray sheets. Soaked to the skin, he pushed ahead, trusting the horse to find solid footing. Progress was agonizingly slow, and thinking about Jessie only made matters worse.

With every mile, his anxiety increased until his pulse broke into a gallop as he rounded the last bend in the trail. The cabin was still above him, hidden from view by rocks, trees and blinding rain. Matt pushed aside the dark premonition that hung over him. Jessie would be all right, he told himself. She would be there, waiting for news, and they would shelter together until the rain stopped. No one, not even Virgil Gates, could expect her to move out in this weather.

Urging on his tired horse, he came up over the lip of the trail and into the clearing where the cabin stood—or where it had stood. The sight that greeted Matt's eyes sucked the breath from his lungs.

The place Jessie had called home lay in charred, crumbling ruins. The sheds and corrals had been burned to ashes. Where the cabin had stood, only a few scattered timbers and the iron stove, with its blackened chimney thrusting skyward, remained.

"Jessie!" He was out of the saddle, shouting frantically. "Jessie! Where are you?"

The words were swallowed by the steady drone of the rain.

Sick with dread, he used a green limb to stir through the sodden ashes of the cabin. He found fire-blackened dishes and heat-warped metal utensils. He found fragments of furniture, burned cloth, buttons and what looked like a twisted boot. But there was no sign of a human body, and Matt breathed a silent prayer of thanks for that.

"Jessie!" He shouted her name again and again, with all his strength. But he knew by now there would be no answer.

Matt widened his search to the sheds and the corral. He found no burned animal remains, not even chickens, which gave him, at least, a little hope. He pictured Jessie releasing the creatures to safety, then torching the ranch to leave Virgil Gates with nothing but charred earth. She was capable of such an act, he knew. But Matt could imagine other, darker scenarios.

He cursed in desperation. If he'd only stayed with her today, none of this would have happened.

Extending his search, he circled the perimeter of the clearing. The storm had begun to clear, but the driving rain had washed the ground clean of tracks. There was nothing to be found. Nothing but mud and ashes.

"Jessie!" His cry echoed off the mountains and died into silence. "Answer me, damn it! Answer me!"

Jessie huddled, shivering, in a dark corner of the old trapper's cabin. The space between the cupboard and the wall was the driest spot she could find, but even here, rain trickled through the sod roof and dripped off the brim of her hat. Her hair was wet; her clothes were wet; her boots were wet, and her teeth chattered uncontrollably. But at least, for now, she was safe.

The men from the Gates Ranch had come after her, but her knowledge of this mountain with its trails, ledges and hollows had saved her. Hiding the packhorse in a secluded box canyon, she'd led the riders on a long chase. In the end, it had been the rain that saved her. Soaked and weary, the riders had turned their backs to the storm and headed for town.

What if she'd been caught? Jessie asked herself now. She was guilty of burning property that was no longer hers.

At the very least, she would have been turned over to the town marshal, jailed and ordered to pay for the damage. But Virgil's hirelings, she sensed, would have found far worse ways to punish her. They would have used her in every possible way, then left her body to rot in the mountains. And Virgil would have turned a blind eye. After all, who was she? She had no property, no money, no family. Who would miss her, or care enough to look for her?

Who, except Matt Langtry?

Jessie huddled deeper into her sodden coat, remembering how Matt's kiss had ignited a bonfire inside her. She remembered how his tender fingers had carried her to the point of straining agony, and beyond, to an explosion of sweet relief. Everything he'd done, everything he'd given her, she had wanted—

his mouth, his hands, on the most intimate parts of her body. Looking back from where she was now, so cold and alone, she knew she would have given him everything if he'd chosen to take it. And after those few waking moments of shame, she would have lived the rest of her life without a flicker of regret.

Had he come back? Was he looking for her now, in the storm? The answer no longer mattered. He was a lawman, and she had broken the law. It would be his sworn duty to find her and bring her in for punishment.

Why couldn't she have met Matt in some ordinary way—at a dance, at church, or in town? Then she might have flirted playfully with him, catching his attention. If he'd chosen to court her, she would have let herself fall deeply and wildly in love with him. She would have been happy to spend her life warming his bed, having his babies and building a life together.

If things had happened that way, maybe Frank would still be alive. Maybe he'd be courting a girl of his own, someone to share the beautiful quilt their mother had made for his bride.

But why dwell on what would never be? Frank was dead, and she was a fugitive. Unless she wanted to risk jail, she could not allow Matt Langtry to cross her path again.

Something stirred behind the woodpile. Jessie's nerves jumped as a pack rat scampered out of the shadows. Unafraid, it settled a few feet from her and began grooming its thick brown fur, cleaning its whiskered face with its tiny paws.

Strangely comforted, Jessie watched the contented little creature. If a pack rat could make a home in this place, so could she. The leaky cabin roof could be patched with fresh sod, the log walls sealed with mud. Years of accumulated grime could be scrubbed away. With summer coming, there would be time to lay in a supply of food and firewood. She could survive here—she *would* survive here.

The storm was clearing at last. The steady drumming of the rain had ebbed to a trickle. Pale fingers of light poked through the holes in the cabin roof. Jessie unfolded her cramped body. Her first movement sent the pack rat scurrying off into the shadows.

Her teeth were still chattering, but despite the stash of dry wood, she dared not make a fire in the rusty stove. The stovepipe was liable be clogged with nests and debris. Worse, Virgil's henchmen could be watching the mountain. A rising plume of smoke could be seen for miles.

Reaching the door, she flung it open to let in air and light. Then she went outside to check the horses. By now the sun was coming out. Water dripped from the eaves of the cabin and glittered in drops, like liquid diamonds, on the fresh spring grass. Chickadees chased each other through the budding aspen trees.

The mare and the pinto were grazing in the trees, where she'd tethered them in the storm. Their coats gleamed with rain. Jessie made a mental note to build them a stout corral as soon as possible. There were wild mustangs in these mountains, and this pair could all too easily break loose and join them.

She had stowed the packed supplies in a hollow under the cabin—a drier place than the cabin itself. Now she dragged the bundle into the open. It was time to take stock of what she'd managed to snatch from the house.

The quilt she'd used to make the bundle was damp and muddy. Since she'd planned to use it for sleeping, it would need to be spread on the bushes in the sun. Once it was dry, the mud could be shaken out of the fabric.

The bundle's contents included a shovel, an ax, a saw, a hammer and a few nails, as well as her good skinning knife, her pistol and two boxes of bullets. These essentials she piled to one side while she went through the flour sacks that she'd stuffed with things from the house.

From the bedroom she'd taken some ragged sheets, two pairs of overalls, two flannel shirts, some underthings and several pairs of socks. Sadly, in her haste, she'd overlooked the comb, brush and looking glass set that had been her mother's, but Jessie had managed to save her mother's sewing box.

The scissors, needles and thread would come in handy.

From the kitchen, she had saved a kettle, a saucepan, a tin cup and a few utensils. The china dishes had been too fragile and heavy to even think of taking. But she had seized a few of her favorite books off the shelf. There was the Bible, of course, as well *Aesop's Fables, The Collected Works of Shakespeare,* and *Great Expectations* by Charles Dickens. The other books, much as she loved them, had been left for the fire.

There was little else except food—a bag of flour, some salt and baking powder, a sack of dried beans, a tin of Arbuckle coffee, a string of dried apples and a few strips of venison jerky. What she had wouldn't last long, Jessie realized with a sinking heart. She could hunt and forage all summer, but sooner or later she would need things from a store—and she had only a few dollars, folded and stashed in her stocking.

But the money problem could wait. Her vow to clear Frank could not. The trail of evidence was getting colder by the day. To find the real killer, she would need to be in the valley—in town or at the Gates Ranch. But how could she watch and listen without being seen? Jessie's fist balled in frustration. If only there were some way for her to become…invisible.

Her heart contracted as her eyes fell on the scissors that lay in her mother's sewing box. For the space of a long breath she stared down at the sharp metal blades. Yes, it was the only way, she told herself. As a woman, she would attract attention anywhere she went. But who would look at a young boy, especially one who was ragged and unkempt, dressed in mud-stained overalls and a drooping hat that hid his face?

Trembling, Jessie snatched up the scissors and, with her free hand, seized a lock of her hair. The steel blades flashed as the first ebony curl fell on the wet grass, where it lay coiled like some dying thing. For a moment Jessie stared down at it, mourning all that had passed from her life. Then, shoving self-pity aside, she reached for another lock of hair and raised the scissors again.

The burial of Allister Gates took place the following day, after a funeral that overflowed the small community church. Matt had decided against sitting through the long, crowded service, but he did join the procession that followed the hearse to the hillside cemetery above town. Mingling with townspeople and visitors would give him a good chance to watch, listen and ask a few questions.

Virgil and Lillian rode behind the hearse in a black-draped open carriage. They sat straight-backed and silent, as if aware of the many eyes watching them. But Matt could not help noticing how Virgil's attention kept flickering toward his sister-in-law.

For a newly bereaved widow, Lillian looked stunning. Her black silk bombazine gown clung to every curve of her hourglass figure. Her red-gold hair was drawn back in a simple bun and crowned by a traditional widow's bonnet with a veil. But when the breeze blew the veil aside, the face behind it was fresh and rosy, the sparkling green eyes undimmed by tears.

Neither she nor Virgil seemed to be in deep mourning. But appearances were one thing. Proof was another. And right now it was all Matt could do to focus his attention on the funeral. Yesterday he'd spent hours searching for Jessie. He'd combed the woods and hillsides for miles around the burned-out ranch, but he'd found no trace of her. If she'd left any kind of tracks behind, the rain had washed them away.

In the hollow down the trail from the ranch, he'd met the neighbors who'd been given her cow and chickens. Mariah Hawkins had told him how Jessie had refused their invitation to stay with them because she had a plan and would be fine on her own. What that plan was, Mrs. Hawkins hadn't been able to learn. But it was clear that she liked Jessie and was deeply worried about her.

As the grave dedication droned on, Matt's focus shifted toward the mountains. Was Jessie up there, hiding out where no one could find her? Or could she be lying somewhere, injured, raped or dead? Although he hadn't met them, Matt had heard about the hired guns who worked for the Gates Ranch. Matt's stomach clenched at the thought of what they might do to a pretty, vulnerable woman like Jessie.

Lord, if only she'd told him where she was going. If only she'd left him some kind of message to let him know she was all right, some clue, even an accidental one.

But maybe she had, Matt realized suddenly. Maybe, the whole time he was searching, it had been right under his nose.

After the funeral he would go back up the mountain. He would look through the ruins again. This time he would take stock, not of what he found, but of what might be missing. Before the fire, he had seen the tools in the shed. He had seen the utensils and other things in the house, things that Jessie would need to survive in the wild on her own. If the metal remains of these objects were missing from the ashes, it would likely mean she'd taken them before setting fire to her own ranch. It wasn't much to go on, but at least it might give him some peace.

The sound of earth hitting the lid of the coffin startled him back to the present. Lillian was turning away from the grave, brushing the dirt from her black kidskin gloves. Virgil followed her, staring down at his brother's coffin before dropping his own handful of rocky Wyoming soil into the hole. Others did the same, but Matt, who was neither a friend nor a relative, did not join in the ritual. Neither, he noticed, did a lean, dark-haired man in a well-tailored suit who stood on the fringe of the crowd.

Something about the stranger—an air of grace and power—drew Matt's attention and held it. As he watched, the man turned around, paused, then walked straight toward him.

The distance between them gave Matt a chance to study the stranger. His skin was a golden mahogany color, his features hawk-sharp, with high cheekbones that suggested Indian blood. A half-breed, maybe Shoshone, Matt guessed. Whoever he was, there was nothing ordinary about him.

As he came within speaking distance, the stranger extended his hand. His eyes were almost black, their gaze direct and confident.

"I make it my business to know every lawman in these parts," he said. "We haven't met. The name is Tolliver. Morgan Tolliver."

Jessie lay belly-flat in a clump of sage, looking downhill toward the cemetery. She had come here to watch the burial, hoping to gain some insight into the circumstances surrounding Allister's death. But she should have known the adventure would be a waste of time. She could recognize people at this distance, but she couldn't see their expressions or hear anything they might be saying. And even if she could have done so, it would have made no difference. From the moment she'd seen Matt arrive, Jessie had been unable to take her eyes off him.

She could see him now, standing a dozen paces from the grave, talking to a man she recognized as Morgan Tolliver. Jessie had visited the Tolliver Ranch with her father a few times to deliver the horses they'd caught and broken. The Tollivers had always treated her family well. She had warm memories of sitting at their huge dinner table, overcome by the rustic beauty of the big log ranch house, the finery of the tableware and the bounty of mouth-watering food, served by the Tollivers' Chinese cook.

Jacob Tolliver, Morgan's father, had been alive then, a gruff, handsome old man whose frail body was confined to a wheelchair. Jessie had not been back to the Tolliver ranch since Jacob's death. But she'd heard that Morgan had married a young widow with a daughter, and had fathered twin boys. The Tolliver Ranch must be a lively place these days, she mused.

But she hadn't come here to remember the Tollivers. And she certainly hadn't come to pine over Matt Langtry. The very fact that Matt was here, mingling with the wealthy ranchers and leading citizens of the county, was enough to set him apart from her. Matt was ambitious. He knew the advantage of having friends in high places. And he was not about to alienate any of these people by looking for a murderer among them.

If Matt played his cards right, he could become a full-fledged U.S. marshal in a few years. From there, anything was possible. He could get a high-placed government job, run for congress, even be elected governor. The right connections would make all the difference—and marriage into a wealthy and powerful family would give him those connections, Jessie reminded herself. The last woman Matthew T. Langtry was apt to wed would be the orphaned daughter of a horse trader with no money, no property, and the threat of arrest hanging over her cropped head.

Matt had chosen his side—and it was not her side. The sooner she forgot him, the safer her heart would be.

Tearing her eyes away from his tall figure, she watched the people leaving the graveside. Virgil and Lillian Gates were moving down the slope together. She was leaning on his arm, her elegant head bending toward his. Could the two of them have been more than in-laws, even while Allister was alive? If the answer was yes, it could provide a powerful motive for murder. Marriage would give Virgil a glamorous wife and Lillian a younger, more virile husband. As a couple, they would own the entire ranch.

Finding Frank's rifle would have given them the perfect chance to kill Allister and put the blame on someone else. But how could she bring them to justice unless she could prove what they'd surely done?

Whatever the risk, she had to learn more.

Biting back his emotions, Matt studied the man who might, or might not, be his half brother. Apart from a similarity in build, there was little resemblance between himself and Morgan Tolliver. Morgan's coloring and his sharp aquiline features had likely come from his Shoshone mother. Looks alone would not tell Matt whether he and this man shared the same blood.

What puzzled Matt now was the way Morgan had singled him out and come straight toward him, as if he'd been waiting for the burial service to end. Clearly the man had something to discuss. But what?

So far, Morgan had made polite conversation, asking Matt where he'd come from and how he liked Wyoming. Matt responded with equal courtesy, waiting for Morgan to get to the heart of what he had to say.

"I understand young Frank Hammond was arrested for Allister's murder," Morgan said abruptly, and Matt felt his heart drop.

"That's right," he hedged. "Frank Hammond's rifle was found near the body. The bullets in the gun matched the one that killed Allister."

Morgan scowled. "I did business with Frank's father for years. Tom Hammond was one of the most honest men I've ever known. You'll never convince me his son's a killer."

"I agree with you there," Matt replied cautiously. "The boy didn't strike me as the sort who'd shoot a man in cold blood."

"I was hoping you'd feel that way," Morgan said. "I've offered to pay for Frank's defense. Tomorrow I'll be meeting with my lawyer in Sheridan. Before we talk to Frank, I'd like to hear your version of what happened."

Matt had hoped to keep Frank's death a secret until he heard from Sheriff Canton. But now, as he faced Morgan Tolliver, he knew the moment of truth had come. Whatever the consequences, he could not lie to this man.

"I'm afraid I have some bad news," he said. "Frank died two days ago on his way to Sheridan. Walk with me down to the horses, and I'll tell you what happened."

Morgan listened in grim silence as the story unfolded. Matt forced himself to be brutally honest, sparing no details. "Frank's death was my fault," he said, knowing it was true. "It was my job to keep the situation under control and get him safely to the county jail. Things got out of hand, and I failed."

Morgan's cold black eyes held neither understanding nor forgiveness. "Then you should take it on yourself to clear the boy. The Hammonds were good people. I'd bet my life their son didn't do this."

"That's what I'm trying to prove. That's why I'm here now."

Morgan glared at him. He was clearly a man who valued action above empty words, and words were all Matt had given him.

"What about Jessie? Where is she?"

Matt felt his heart clench at the mention of her name. "Missing. Her cabin is gone, burned. I'm hoping she did it herself to spite Virgil, and that she's hiding in the mountains. Otherwise…" Matt could not even voice the other, darker possibility.

"Find her." Morgan's look would have withered stone. "When you do, tell her she has a place with my family, on our ranch, for as long as she wants it. If she's too proud to come as a guest, tell her we can use her help with the horses."

"I'll find her."

"See that you do, Marshal." Morgan donned his Stetson, untied his tall roan from the hitching rail and swung into the saddle. "Sheriff Canton will know where to get in touch with me. I'll be seeing him tomorrow. Do you want me to tell him what happened to Frank?"

"He should know by now. I wired him this morning, as soon as the telegraph office was open. I'll be back in Sheridan as soon as I've finished my business here." Matt squinted up into the sunlight, which had transformed Morgan into a towering black silhouette. "Canton will want a piece of my hide, I expect."

"He'll take it. Count on that." Morgan tipped his hat, wheeled his horse and rode away.

Feeling like a whipped dog, Matt watched him canter the horse down the road and vanish around the bend. Only now that he'd failed did he realize how badly he'd wanted to win Morgan's approval. Maybe he'd been too honest about what had happened. Maybe he should have glossed over Frank's death, blamed it on the vigilantes, then tried to steer the conversation toward something pleasant. But no, he sensed Morgan would have seen right through him. He'd had no choice except to tell the raw, unpolished truth.

But what difference did it make now? It was too late to change anything that had happened. As for Morgan's being his half brother, the whole idea was best forgotten. Even if the blood tie could be proved, Morgan would never accept him, let alone welcome him. His manner had made that clear enough.

Turning away from the road, Matt mounted his horse. He'd wasted enough time brooding. What mattered now was tracking down Jessie and bringing her safely back to the Tolliver Ranch.

Morgan Tolliver had offered her a new home and a new life with friends who were powerful enough to protect her. But if Jessie was alive, she could be playing a dangerous game. Everything hinged on his finding her before she took one chance too many.

Chapter Ten

A gibbous moon, waning from fullness, hung like an unplucked peach above the eastern plain. The wail of a coyote quivered through the darkness as Jessie crept along the fence line. The grass beneath her thin boots was cold and wet.

She'd spent the afternoon hiding in the hills above the Gates Ranch, watching the funeral guests come and go. The two-story ranch house appeared grander than she remembered, with a newly finished portico standing where the front porch had been. Today the portico was elegantly draped in yards of black bunting—Lillian Gates's idea, Jessie surmised. Virgil certainly wouldn't have thought of it. He and Allister had lived like bachelor cowboys before she came into their lives. It would take a woman with expensive tastes and a strong, demanding will to make such changes.

And now, perhaps, Lillian had made the biggest change of all.

Ranchers had come from all over the county for the funeral. Many of them had stopped by the house afterward to visit and enjoy a meal of barbecued beef. Jessie had watched for Matt, but he hadn't shown up. Neither had Morgan Tolliver. As the afternoon faded into twilight, she had crawled back into the trees, curled up beneath a clump of willows and fallen into a restless sleep.

Now, with the darkness around her, she was fully awake. At the end of the drive, she could see the house. The guests had long since left, taking the horses and carriages that had crowded the yard. Now only two lamplit rooms were visible from the front of the house. The downstairs light, she calculated, would be coming from the front hall. The lighted room upstairs, to the left of the portico, was undoubtedly a bedroom, either Lillian's or Virgil's.

Gauging the moon's height above the horizon, Jessie reckoned that it was a little after ten o'clock. The tired servants would have long since cleaned up after the meal and gone to bed. Lillian and Virgil would be alone.

Were the two of them lovers? That was what Jessie had come to find out.

She paused as she crept past the barn, with its attached corral. This, she knew, was where Allister Gates had died.

Dropping to a crouch, she settled herself against the corral fence, where a dozen horses drowsed in the moonlight. She tried to picture Frank coming out of the barn leading the stallion as Allister emerged from the house with his pistol. How scared Frank must have been. The stallion was a skittish, sensitive animal. As Allister came close, Frank's fear alone could have made the horse nervous enough to rear.

Where had Allister fallen? And where had he died? If she'd known that much, at least, she might have been able to search the ground for evidence. But what was she thinking? The ground where Allister died had been trampled and rained on for the past three days. There would be nothing left to find.

And there was no one to help her, she realized. Frank was gone and Matt Langtry was out of her reach. She was groping in the dark, with nothing to go on except Frank's story.

When she looked toward the house again, she saw that the light on the first floor had gone out. Only the glow in the upstairs bedroom remained. If she wanted to see what was happening inside the room, she would have to get high enough to look through the second-floor window.

Moving carefully to the foot of a tall pine tree that grew on the east side of the house, she spat on her hands, crouched and sprang for a lower limb. Swinging hard, she caught a higher, sturdier limb with her feet and pulled herself up until she could sit on it. The tree was even rougher than she'd feared. By now her hands were bleeding, but never mind, she was almost high enough to see over the sill. A few more grinding inches and she was there.

The shutters were open, and there were no blinds on the window. Only a thin lace curtain veiled Jessie's view of the room. She could see the lamp with its rose-tinted glass shade sitting on the night table. A few steps away, Lillian sat at the dresser in a peach satin robe, brushing her glorious red-gold hair.

She was alone.

Feeling foolish, Jessie slid lower, but the strap on her overalls had caught on a sharp limb. She was straining upward, trying to get it loose, when the bedroom door opened from the hall to reveal Virgil, clad in a dark woolen dressing gown.

Jessie stared, half-afraid to believe her eyes as he walked into the room, moved behind Lillian and put his hands on her shoulders. There it was—had to be—the reason that Allister had died. If Lillian and Virgil were lovers, that would give them every reason to want Allister dead. Now all she needed was a way to connect them to his murder.

Intent on the scene before her, Jessie didn't see the huge owl, flying in to roost, until its wing struck her cheek. Startled, she flung up her arm to shield her eyes. If the owl hadn't been gripping a gopher in its massive talons, it could have ripped her arm or torn a gash in her face. As it was, the creature went at her with its snapping beak and powerful wings, trying to drive her out of the tree.

Struggling wildly to protect herself, Jessie lost her hold. Down, down she slid, grabbing at limbs to slow her fall. Bark scraped her. Limbs and needles jabbed her. She clenched her teeth against the pain, biting back a scream as she crashed to the ground.

For a moment she lay stunned and bleeding on the thick bed of pine needles that had cushioned her fall. Then she heard the front door open and saw the flash of a lantern from the portico.

"Who's there?" Virgil's voice bawled. "Come on out in the light before I pull this trigger and blow your damnfool head off!"

Any second, Jessie knew, he'd be coming around the house. Torn between hiding and running, she chose to run.

Disregarding the pain that shot through her bruised body, she scrambled to her feet and raced for the scrub oak that grew in clumps behind the house. To run in the open on this moonlit night would be to risk a bullet or a crippling blast of buckshot.

She glimpsed the light swinging around the corner of the house. If Virgil fired his gun, the whole ranch would be awake. She could only hope his desire to be alone with Lillian would outweigh the need to chase down an intruder.

Flattening herself under a bushy oak, she lay still, listening as Virgil rummaged beneath the pine tree. The pine needles wouldn't show her tracks clearly, thank heaven, but he would see the spot where she'd landed on the needles. If he checked the sharp, broken branches he would likely find blood or shreds of her torn shirt and overalls.

He was moving again. Jessie could see the light of the swinging lantern as he prowled the yard. She held her breath as he walked within a stone's throw of where she lay. Her heart crept into her throat as he paused, swung the lantern in a sweeping arc and moved on. Thank goodness the family didn't keep dogs around the house. A dog's sharp nose would have found her in seconds.

"I know you're out there, you bastard!" Virgil snarled into the shadows. "Come on out now, and I might let you live!"

Jessie lay frozen against the leafy ground. She could feel something crawling along her leg. She hoped to heaven it wasn't a rattlesnake. Closing her eyes, she moved her lips in a silent prayer.

At last, with a grunt of disgust, Virgil moved on. Jessie could hear the crunch of his boots as he walked the rest of the way around the house and mounted the steps of the portico. Even after she heard the front door close, she lay still, knowing he could still be there, waiting for her to come out into the open.

Only when she saw the light in the upstairs window flicker and go out did she dare to move. The crawling sensation along her leg had gone away. Maybe she'd only imagined it. But she could feel danger all around her in the night.

Making a wide circle through the scrub, Jessie cut back toward the road. Her left ankle was beginning to swell. A bad sprain, she guessed. But she couldn't take time to stop and look at it. She needed to get back to the horse she'd left hidden in the hills above town. She needed to get home, if the leaky little cabin in the high meadow could be called a home.

The shortest route back to the horse would take her straight through town. On any other night, Jessie wouldn't have gone that way, but the hour was late and her ankle screamed with every step. The longer path, which cut through the cemetery, would add at least another mile to the trek. In her condition, she knew she'd never make it that far.

The stores and offices along Main Street were dark and silent. Only the saloon, which spilled a pool of light through its swinging doors, contained any life at this hour. Drunken laughter, the clink of glasses and the slap of cards on a wooden table trickled through the darkness as Jessie limped past on the opposite side of the muddy road. The place would be closing soon. She didn't want to be here when the saloon emptied its customers into the night.

As she passed the general store, she glimpsed a bedraggled figure moving alongside her in the moonlit glass. Jessie gasped, then bit back nervous laughter as she realized she was looking at her own reflection. Her wild tumble from the tree, with its bumps, scrapes and scratches, had perfected her disguise. She looked like a ragged, homeless beggar boy who'd been beaten and kicked from door to door, bitten by dogs and pelted by mud. Her own dear mother wouldn't have known her.

She knew she should move on, but a poster in the lower corner of the window seized her attention. Printed in block letters below the silhouette of a galloping horse was the following notice:

SHERIDAN OPENING HORSE RACE
$50 Prize, Winner Take All
May 20, Two o'clock p.m.,
Sheridan Race Course
Picnic to Follow

The monthly horse race was a regular event from late spring to early fall. This race, which was ten days off, would be the first of the season. Pausing a few seconds longer, Jessie tucked the date and time into her memory, although she no longer had reason to do so. Frank had been planning to race Midnight and win some much-needed cash, but now neither he nor the stallion would ever race again.

Tearing her eyes from the poster, Jessie moved closer to the window. The interior of the store was dark, but Jessie had been inside so many times that her mind held an exact picture of the goods on their shelves—canned meats, fruits and vegetables, dry beans and rice, bullets, tools, salves and bandages and medicines—things she desperately needed.

How easy would it be to creep around to the back and find a way inside? She wouldn't take much—just some ointment for her scratches, maybe a few nails and bullets, a comb, some salt…

But what was she thinking? She was no thief. If she wanted more supplies, she would get them the honest way—with money. And she would get the money honestly as well, Jessie vowed. If only she could find a way.

"You! Boy!" The gruff shout rasped out of the darkness behind her. Spinning around, Jessie saw three men coming out of the saloon and into the street. Her legs went watery beneath her as she recognized the roughnecks who worked for Virgil Gates.

"Boy! You stealin' something? You even thinkin' about it? We're gonna fix you good!"

They laughed as they pounded toward her, splashing through the mud. The fact that they'd been drinking made them all the more dangerous. If they got their hands on her and discovered she wasn't a boy at all…

Fear shot energy into her tortured limbs. Leaping away, she sprinted around the store and into the alley between the store and the boardinghouse next door. The strain on her ankle was excruciating, but she was too terrified to feel it. She ran for her life, dodging among the discarded boxes, crates and refuse that littered the narrow space. Her pursuers lumbered after her, enjoying the sport. If only she'd brought her pistol—but no, it was just as well. Even with a weapon, she couldn't take on three experienced gunfighters and expect to come out alive.

Jessie could feel her strength ebbing. If she couldn't find a hiding place, they would simply run her down, chasing her until she dropped.

Ahead of her, the alley ended at the rear of the store. She would round the corner ahead of the three men. For a few seconds she would be out of sight. Those seconds could provide the only chance of saving herself.

A six-foot stack of empty wooden crates stood against the side of the store. Risking precious time, she pushed at the crates, knocking them over behind her as she ran. She heard a crash and a vile curse, but she dared not look back to see what was happening.

Rounding the corner, she saw a big tin laundry tub propped against the back of the boardinghouse. Without pausing to think, she dived under it and pulled it down over her body. Curled on her side with her head against her knees, Jessie filled the entire space beneath the tub. There was scarcely any air to breathe, let alone room to expand her lungs. Confined places had always bothered her. Already, after only seconds, her nerves were screaming for air and space.

The ground quivered beneath her as the three men came pounding around the building. They paused, swearing. The tub muffled their words, but Jessie sensed that they were standing right next to her.

"Now where did the little bastard go?" Jessie recognized the cultured voice of the gunman called Ringo.

Jessie heard a belch and a raw laugh before a second voice answered. "Hell, we probably scared the little bugger to death. Come on, let's get back to the ranch. Mr. Virgil wants us up at first light to start the brandin'."

"Sure, now, Lem," a third voice interjected. "And if you was in Mr. Virgil's shoes, would *you* be up at first light?"

The question was greeted with raucous, ribald laughter that grew distant, then faded into stillness.

Were they gone? Teeth chattering, Jessie huddled against the cold mud beneath the wash tub. Unless she'd heard wrong, the men had hinted that they knew about Virgil and Lillian. If questioned forcefully enough, they might be able to back up what she'd seen with her own eyes. But she was the last person who could approach Virgil's hired ruffians. Such a dangerous errand called for someone stronger. Someone like Matt Langtry.

But Matt would be off somewhere with his powerful friends by now, she told herself. Why should he try to prove Frank's innocence when it would cast his own reputation in a bad light? She could not count on him, or anyone else, for help.

Risking a slight movement, she eased up the edge of the tub and gulped the fresh night air into her lungs. For a few moments she lay there, terrified of emerging from her hiding place. If the three men were close enough to see or hear her, she would get no second chance.

At last, when nothing happened, she raised the tub, uncurled her cramped body and crawled out into the open. The town was dark and quiet now, the only sign of life a skinny dog sniffing at the rubbish in the alley. It raised its head as Jessie crept past, but made no sound. For that, at least, she was grateful.

The pinto was waiting in the overgrown box canyon where she'd left it. Jessie dragged herself wearily into the saddle and sagged over the horse's neck. The cabin was a long way off, and the narrow trail, which wound through heavy timber, over rock slides and along steep ledges, would be dangerous at night.

She stroked her pinto's mottled neck, grateful for its calm presence and rock-steady gait. As the path wound upward, her head began to droop. The past few days had been all she could bear, and now the strain was catching up with her. She was exhausted.

For the first few miles, where the trail wound among the high ledges, Jessie forced herself to stay awake. She sang every song she'd ever learned, from church hymns to bar ballads, making up words where her memory failed. She recited the poems she'd learned in school, such as "The boy stood on the burning deck…" When all else failed, she pinched her own cheeks until they stung.

For a time her tactics worked. But as the path leveled out into upland meadows and forests, she could feel herself slipping into a delicious fog. Matt's image seemed to float before her, his eyes tender and filled with yearning. She could feel his arms around her, cradling her close as he had that night in the cabin. His mouth found hers, and she drifted with him, drowning blissfully in his kisses as she dreamed of the years they would have together. She would stay with him, love him. As long as he was at her side, she would have the courage to face whatever life brought them.

Only then, as the rosy mist began to clear, did she happen to glance down. She and Matt were standing on a narrow ledge, with a black empty space yawning below them.

Now, suddenly, there were cruel hands, evil hands, seizing her body and limbs, tearing her away from Matt's embrace. She clung to him as the dark force pulled them apart. Finger by desperate finger, she lost him. As she tumbled into darkness, the last thing she saw was his face. Strangely, he was smiling.

Jessie opened her eyes to a chilly dawn. She was lying on her back in the long grass, gazing up through the budding branches of an aspen. Above her, the clouds streaked the pewter sky with shades of amethyst, rose and amber.

Dazed and disoriented, she lay there blinking into the pale light. The dream lingered around her like a shroud.

Her mother, a true believer in dreams, would have warned her to heed this one. But what did it mean? Nothing good; Jessie was certain of that. But was it a warning that Matt would betray her if she turned to him? Or had she woven the dream herself, from the warp of her fears and the weft of her yearnings?

The calls of awakening birds filled her ears as she struggled to sit up. The slightest motion shot agony through her beaten body. What had she done to herself?

The breathy snort of a horse, coming from just beyond her head, jerked Jessie wide awake. Had she been followed? A grunt of pain exploded between her teeth as she rolled over into a crouch, ready to fight or run.

But it was only the pinto standing over her, its soft white muzzle almost brushing her face. Fifty yards away, across the grassy meadow, she could see the run-down trapper's cabin with her mare securely tethered outside.

Overcome by emotion, she flung her arms around the pinto's neck and pressed her face against its warm cheek.

"Spade, you dear old rascal!" she whispered. "You brought me home! You'd probably have put me to bed if you'd known how, wouldn't you?"

The distant nicker of another horse reached her ears. That would be Gypsy, wanting attention, Jessie thought. She had always spoiled the beautiful mare.

Untangling herself from Spade, she rose gingerly to her feet. She could see Gypsy dancing anxiously at the end of her tether, but the mare was paying no heed to her mistress. Her whole body was straining toward something at the far side of the clearing.

Rubbing the sleep from her eyes, Jessie followed the direction of the mare's agitated gaze. Only then did she see them, emerging like ghosts from the misted trees into the meadow—the green-broken mustangs she'd freed from the ranch.

She watched them fan out into the long grass, ears pricking, nostrils flaring. One of the mares, who'd been about to foal, had a tiny colt at her side, a gangly little blue roan that melted Jessie's heart the instant she set eyes on it.

Holding out her hand, Jessie whistled softly, trying to coax them closer. They nickered and stretched their necks toward her, as if expecting a treat, but they kept their distance, as if held back by some unseen force.

Then, as the savage, bugling scream reached her ears, thrilling her to the marrow of her bones, Jessie understood.

Her gaze followed the sound to a sight that stopped her heart. Standing guard on a knoll above the meadow, mane and tail bannering in the wind, was the black stallion.

Chapter Eleven

The storms had moved on, leaving the plains and mountains carpeted in green velvet. Lupine and Indian paintbrush dotted the hillsides. Clover, violets and buttercups flowered on the plains. On the high slopes below the pines, the aspen groves were fully leafed and the columbines were coming into bloom. The late spring days were warm, the skies a blazing, cloudless blue.

In Sheridan, the day of the opening race had arrived. The first race day was always a festive time. After the long, isolating winter, it provided a chance for ranch families and townspeople to gather, relax and celebrate.

The morning was set aside for travel and preparation. At two o'clock the races were held on a patch of open flatland outside town. The picnic, with games, music and a charity bake sale, went on all afternoon, followed by a dance that lasted into the night.

For Matt, this would be the first chance to see so many citizens of his district together. Meeting and observing people was important. The more he knew about his neighbors, the easier his job would be when some problem arose among them.

On a whim, he'd entered himself and Copper in the race. The big chestnut had power and speed and loved nothing better than to outrun every horse in sight. If they won, Matt figured on making a few friends by donating his fifty-dollar prize to the fund for the new school building. Even if they lost, the race would give him one more way to make new acquaintances.

All in all, he expected to have a good day—except for two troubling matters that gnawed at him constantly. He'd found no more clues to the murder of Allister Gates and—even more unsettling—he'd failed to find Jessie.

After the funeral he'd ridden back to the burned-out ranch and searched through the ashes. His hunch had been correct. Jessie had cleared out, he'd concluded with dizzying relief. And the empty kerosene jug in the yard confirmed that she'd likely torched the place herself.

He had searched for her until darkness forced him out of the mountains. Even on the damp, muddy ground, he'd found no hoofprints leading away. The earlier storm would have washed them out when she left, he realized. And judging from the evidence, she hadn't come back.

Duty had called him back to Sheridan the next day. But everywhere he went her memory had haunted him. He'd caught imaginary glimpses of her walking down the street, browsing in the General Store, and riding away from him in the twilight. He'd begun to curse the times he started at the sight of a petite figure or a head of dark curls, only to realize he was staring at a stranger.

Even now, Matt scanned the midday crowd. Looking for Jessie had become a habit that, he feared, would stay with him for the rest of his life.

He'd been looking for Morgan Tolliver as well, even though he was braced for the cold rebuff that would come when Morgan learned there was no news. Now, however, it was getting close to race time, and there was still no sign of Morgan. Maybe something had kept the Tollivers at home, Matt reasoned.

As he turned down a side street toward the livery stable, where he'd left orders to have Copper saddled and waiting, he heard a shout.

"Marshal Langtry!"

Matt swung around as a husky female voice called out to him. To his surprise, he saw Lillian and Virgil hurrying toward him. Virgil wore shirtsleeves and a leather vest, but Lillian was dressed in full widow's regalia, complete with a black parasol. He'd never seen a woman look so radiant in mourning, Matt observed wryly. Widowhood must agree with her.

On his first full day back in Sheridan, he'd wired the U.S. Marshal's office in St. Louis, asking them to have someone check the history of the woman who'd married Allister Gates last summer. He'd had his suspicions about Lillian all along. A look at the woman's past might tell him whether those suspicions were well-founded. But time had passed, and he'd heard nothing back. Maybe he ought to contact them again, he thought as she hurried toward him.

"We've been…wanting to…talk with you, Marshal." Lillian was out of breath. Her bosom heaved becomingly. "It seems we've had a prowler at our house."

"A prowler?" Matt felt his stomach clench in dread of what was coming next. "What sort of prowler?"

"Nobody I've seen," Virgil said grimly. "But whoever it is, he's been to the house at least twice. The night after the funeral he climbed a tree outside Lillian's bedroom window. When I heard him and came outside with a shotgun, he ran. The second time was just a few nights ago. I didn't hear anything, but there were tracks under the windows, like somebody'd been trying to look in."

"What sort of tracks?" Matt asked, sick with the certainty of what he'd hear next.

"Small. Like this," Virgil grunted, indicating the length between his two big hands. "Some kid, I'd bet, sneaking around, looking for something to steal or a chance to spy on a woman."

"Have you talked to Heber Sims?" Matt forced his face to assume a look of calm concern. "As Felton's marshal, I'd think he'd be the one to handle this."

"Heber?" Virgil snorted. "Hell, that old geezer couldn't catch a one-legged rooster! You were out to our place asking questions before the funeral. We figured you might have some ideas."

"I was looking into a murder. It shouldn't take a U.S. Deputy Marshal to chase down a prowling boy." Matt spoke around the knot in his throat. It had to be Jessie who was spying on the house. Lord, if he could get his hands on the woman and shake some sense into her…

"We heard what happened to that horrid boy who shot Allister," Lillian said. "You knew he was dead when you came to see us. Why didn't you tell us then?"

"Because I hadn't yet reported it to the sheriff," Matt responded brusquely. By now, Frank's death was public knowledge, and he'd taken his own licks for losing a prisoner. Lillian's question was natural enough, but her demanding tone irritated him.

"Didn't Frank Hammond have a sister?" Lillian asked. "I recall seeing a dark-haired girl with him in town. Pretty little thing, for a common sort. Maybe you should have arrested her, too, as an accomplice."

"There was no reason to detain Miss Hammond," Matt said stiffly.

"No reason, hell!" Virgil exploded. "She burned down that ranch—burned down my property! I was planning to put the place up for sale. Now it's just ashes, and the land isn't worth spit!"

"Do you have any proof she did it?" Matt spoke above the pounding in his ears.

"Proof! The place was on fire when my boys came up to look things over. They saw her riding away. Chased her all over the blamed mountain. Finally lost her in the rain! Just let me get my hands on that little bitch! I'll show you proof, Marshal!"

"First race in five minutes!" The bullhorn call echoed down the street. People who'd lingered too long shopping and visiting rushed toward the race grounds. Virgil seemed ready to bolt with them, but Lillian lingered, her hand firmly gripping his sleeve.

"About that prowler, Marshal—" she began, but Matt cut her off.

"As long as he's just a boy, and he's not doing any harm, I'd say, don't worry about him. Cover your windows at night. When he gets tired of having nothing to see, he'll likely stop coming around."

Lillian's smile was artificially bright. "That sounds like sensible advice, Marshal. Thank—"

"Come on, Lil! We'll miss the race." Virgil's size and momentum were dragging her away. Matt watched them go, his gut churning. At least he knew Jessie was alive. But the rest of the news was even worse than he'd feared. She was living like a hunted animal, playing hide-and-seek with some dangerous people. He had to find her and get her to the Tolliver Ranch before she took one chance too many and found herself up to her pretty ears in trouble.

His first impulse was to dash off and start scouring the mountains, but he'd done that before. This time he'd have to play it smarter, pick up her trail somehow or set a trap. Maybe he should offer to help Virgil and Lillian with their prowler after all. But right now, Matt reminded himself, he had a race to run.

There would be three qualifying quarter-mile heats before the final race. Matt had drawn the third heat, so he still had time to get to the race course. But because of Virgil and Lillian he would miss seeing the first race. As he mounted his horse, the distant gunshot, followed by wild cheering, told him that race was already over.

By the time Matt reached the racing ground, riders were lining up for the second heat. Spectators, many of whom had bets going, clustered in droves around the track. Horses milled behind them, snorting and dancing. Farther back, out of harm's way, the bake-sale booths were set up, and families picnicked on the grass. Where the wagons and buggies ringed the vast meadow, children played tag while horses drowsed in their traces.

There were eight riders in the second heat. Two of them would qualify for the final race. The starting gun popped, and eight horses exploded down the track. The quarter-mile race, run at breakneck speed, lasted less than half a minute. The crowd whooped as the two cowboys who'd led all the way turned and rode back down the track, grinning and waving their Stetsons.

Matt's heat was next. Wrenching his thoughts away from Jessie, he struggled to focus on the race. He felt Copper tense with anticipation as the riders lined up. The big chestnut loved to run and seemed to know exactly what to expect.

The riders leaned forward in their saddles and took off at the starting gun. Matt gave Copper his head and let him run his race. They sailed over the finish line a half-length ahead of the second-place horse.

Matt glimpsed money changing hands as they trotted back toward the starting line. He could see Virgil at the side of the track, standing next to Lillian.

"Marshal!" Virgil called out. "How much d'you want for that horse?"

Matt forced a grin as he rode past. "I'd sooner sell my own brother—if I had a brother!"

Virgil had to be wishing he had the black stallion to race today, Matt mused. If Frank and Jessie hadn't reclaimed the horse, this would have been a day of triumph for the Gates Ranch. Even Copper, fast as he was, would be hard put to hold his own against that four-legged bundle of black lightning. Jessie had been right to set the stallion free. No man who craved fine horses could lay eyes on the creature without wanting it. To possess such a horse, some men would kill—and some would die.

Would a man do the same for a woman? Glancing behind him, Matt saw that Virgil was resting his hand against the small of Lillian's back. Allister had been dead for less than a fortnight, and the two of them were already showing affection in public. But that alone proved nothing. They could be sleeping in the same bed—and likely were. But that didn't make them murderers. Except for Jessie's version of what had happened, the evidence still pointed to Frank Hammond—or to Jessie herself.

The call went up for the final heat, the run for the money. Still preoccupied, Matt wheeled Copper into place at the starting line. Horses danced and snorted. The picnic blankets were deserted as the crowd pressed close to the track.

Struggling to focus on the race, Matt glanced up and down the line of horses and riders. On his right were the two cowboys who'd placed in the second heat. On his left was a well-dressed older man, most likely a rancher, whose horse had finished behind Copper in the third.

The two winners of the first race, which Matt had missed, were on the far left. With the rancher and his horse blocking Matt's view, they were more difficult to see. On the near side, he could make out a wiry, blond cowboy. In the leftmost place was a scruffy farm boy. Dressed in patched overalls and a muddy felt hat, he was mounted on a buckskin mare that seemed far too fine for such a poor lad.

Matt's mouth went dry as he recognized the mare and the slight, bedraggled figure in the saddle. He swore under his breath.

He was looking at Jessie.

Jessie hunched lower over Gypsy's neck, making herself as small as she could. What had possessed her to think she could ride into Sheridan, win the race, collect her prize money and gallop away without being recognized? True, she needed the cash badly, and could think of no other honest way to get it. But desperation must have clouded her judgment. Now it was too late to hide.

Nervously she pulled Gypsy back a few inches, hiding behind the two riders who separated her from Matt. She had hoped he might be busy, or at least that she'd be able to avoid him. But she should have

known better. Not only had Matt seen her—and undoubtedly recognized her—she was actually racing
against him.

Tensing her body, she waited for the starter to
raise his pistol. She'd held Gypsy back in the first
race, deliberately coming in behind the blond cowboy. This time the mare would be running full out.

Gypsy wasn't as fast as the black stallion, but she
was fast enough. Jessie had watched the other horses
run, and she felt confident her mare, a blooded quarter horse, could outrace them—all except for Matt's
superb gelding. Gypsy was as agile as a cat, but the
rangy chestnut had the advantage in power and
length of stride. On a longer track, Matt's horse
would soon have outpaced her. But in this short race,
Jessie calculated, the mare had at least an even
chance.

She could feel Matt's gaze on her as she leaned
into the stirrups, waiting. Part of her, she realized,
had *wanted* to see him today, had hungered to see
him. But now that he was here, she didn't even trust
herself to meet his eyes.

As if things weren't bad enough already, she
glimpsed the flutter of a black parasol and saw Virgil
and Lillian standing at the edge of the track. Jessie's
heart plummeted. The pair didn't know her well and
wouldn't recognize Gypsy. But she knew Lillian had
seen her with Frank in town. If they got a good look

at her, even her cropped hair might not be enough to disguise the fact that she was Frank's sister.

Cold sweat trickled between her flat-bound breasts as the starter pointed his pistol at the sky. Run the race, that was all she could do. She tensed, feeling Gypsy's taut body beneath her. Then, at the sound of the shot, they were off.

The mare's lightning start put her ahead of the other horses, but Matt's big chestnut was moving up even with them. She could see him out of the corner of her eye as they thundered neck and neck down the quarter-mile track. Jessie pressed forward, urging the mare to a blazing gallop. But now, seconds from the finish line, the gelding was easing ahead, and Jessie knew that Gypsy had no more to give. They were going to lose the race by a nose.

She risked a glance toward Matt. Amazingly, she saw that he was pulling back, slowing his horse just enough to let her gain the lead.

The crowd screamed as the mare sprinted across the finish line, barely a hand's breadth ahead of the gelding. On their flanks, the other racers thundered past. Jessie had won the race. But it was a hollow victory.

Gypsy had slowed to a dancing walk. Matt hovered nearby, but Jessie refused to look at him. A horse race was an affair of honor, and his letting her win was the ultimate insult to her own prowess as a rider and Gypsy's prowess as a horse. Oh, yes, let the little woman win. Toss her a few crumbs, then watch her fall at your feet! He must be feeling wonderful about himself right now!

The crowd pressed close as the mayor stepped forward with the leather pouch in his hand—the pouch that contained the traditional prize of five ten-dollar gold eagles. He held it out to Jessie. "Congratulations, young man," he boomed. "Well done!"

Jessie's gaze dropped to her hands, white-knuckled where they clutched the reins. *Don't be a fool!* her practical side argued. *Take the money! You need it! That's why you came!*

Everyone was looking at her, waiting. She was beginning to feel sick. The mayor's florid face with its thick, curling mustache swam before her eyes. She could feel Matt's presence behind her. Oh, why had he done this to her? Why couldn't he have left well enough alone?

In her side vision, she could see Virgil and Lillian standing near the front of the crowd. Only then did she realize that her hat had blown back and was hanging behind her shoulders. Any minute now, they'd be liable to recognize her.

Cold panic welled in Jessie's throat. Her eyes shifted like a trapped animal's, frantic to find an escape. Why had she come here today? She couldn't take the money, couldn't stay. All she wanted was to get out of this place.

Seeing a thin spot in the crowd, she swung her horse and pushed her way through. The mayor gaped after her, the leather pouch still dangling from his fingers.

"What do you think you're doing, boy?" He shouted after her. "Come back here!"

Jessie paid him no attention. The open, grassy flat lay before her. Beyond that was the road back to the mountains—her mountains, her refuge.

She dug her heels into the mare's flanks and they shot toward the hills.

"I'll take that!" Matt snatched the money pouch from the mayor's hand, swung up onto his horse and charged after Jessie at a gallop. She had only a narrow head start on him, and he felt confident that he could catch her. But he didn't want to do it within sight of the curious townspeople. He was more interested in getting her alone, or better yet, trailing her to her secret lair. The lady owed him an explanation, and he didn't want any interruptions.

He held Copper in check for the first few miles, letting her get a comfortable lead as the trail wound up through the sage-covered hills and into the aspen forests. For now, at least, she was simply trying to outrun him, making no effort to hide her tracks. But Matt knew that when her mount began to tire, she'd be apt to take evasive action. Matt was an experienced tracker, but Jessie had grown up in these mountains and knew every foot of them. Trailing her would be a challenge. He would have to be alert for every trick.

Frankly, he was looking forward to the contest.

The sight of her in the lineup for the race had jolted him. Sheridan was the last place he'd expected to see her. She must have been desperate for cash to come to such a public gathering. Well, she was going to get the money she'd won, and she was going to take it, blast her, if he had to cram every coin into her stubborn little—"

But now he was getting emotional, Matt cautioned himself. In dealing with Jessie, he would need to keep a cool head—easier said than done, when just being around her strained his self-control to the breaking point. Where the ladies were concerned, Matt had always prided himself on being a gentleman. But maddening Jessie Hammond could shatter his composure with a flash of her gentian eyes and transform him into a beast with a word. As for those soft lips and that devil-made body…even now, the memory of her quivering release in his arms caused him to swell against the saddle.

Matt cursed out loud, purpling the air as he vented his frustration. Here he was, galloping after a woman in a fever of lust, something he'd never done before in his life. But if that was his reason for chasing Jessie, he needed to stop and turn back right now. Unless he could do his duty—give her the money, escort her to the Tolliver Ranch and walk away—he'd be doing them both more harm than good.

Ahead, he could see where she'd turned her mare off the trail and headed up the slope toward the creek. Oldest tactic in the book, he observed. She would ride upstream, letting the water cover her tracks until she found a good place to come out onto the bank. Trailing her would be a simple matter of finding the spot where she left the creek.

A smile tightened his lips as he guided Copper along the clear line of hoofprints. In his career as a lawman, Matt had tracked down outlaws and renegades who knew every evasive trick ever devised. Following one small woman should be easy enough. Shouldn't it?

Jessie lay flat at the top of an overhanging ledge, peering down at the slope below. Her keen eyes inspected the clumps of spruce and aspen and the rocky escarpments that rose among them. She could see no movement; nor could she hear any sound except the twitter of birds, the rush of the nearby waterfall, and the soft nicker of her mare, waiting in the trees a dozen yards behind her.

Praise be, had she finally lost him?

She had spent most of the afternoon trying to throw Matt off her trail. She had cut across streams and rock slides, laid false tracks, zigzagged and doubled back on her own path. Once he'd passed within a stone's throw of the place where she was hiding, but he'd discovered her trick minutes later. She had barely gotten away without being caught.

Matt was a superb tracker; there was no denying that. But Jessie had learned from the best, her father. She and Frank had grown up playing their own version of hide-and-seek in the mountains, taking turns at tracking and evasion. No one could catch her when she didn't want to be caught.

So why didn't she want to be caught now? Was it because she knew Matt would try to give her the prize money, and she was too proud to take it? Was it because he might arrest her for arson and haul her back to Sheridan in handcuffs, the way he'd taken Frank? Was it because she hated him? Or was it because she was afraid *not* to hate him?

The searing moments she'd spent in Matt's arms had left her raw and vulnerable. Those feelings had come rushing back when she saw him at the race. Right then, she'd known that she couldn't face him. He had too much power over her—power to crush and wound and shame her. Running was the only way to protect herself.

But now the sun was hanging low in the sky, streaking the clouds with the first blush of color. In less than an hour twilight would be setting in, and she was still several miles from the cabin. She was not anxious to be stranded in these ledges after dark, especially with Gypsy. There was too much danger from unseen drop-offs, not to mention wolves and cougars.

Matt would be stranded, too, unless he'd given up and turned back. She could only hope she'd lost him. Either way, it was time to head for the shelter of the cabin.

"Jessie!" Matt's voice echoed from the hollow. "I know you're up there! Stop this crazy game and come down here before you get hurt! Now!" He sounded weary, frustrated and plain mad. Jessie kept her silence, still hoping he'd give up and leave.

"I've got a message for you! It's good news! You'll want to hear it!"

His voice came from somewhere below her, close to the base of the cliffs. She inched forward, trying to look down and see him through the heavy screen of brush. It had to be a trick, she told herself. If he really had a message, why didn't he just give it to her?

"Blast it, woman, answer me!" His furious shout echoed off the canyon walls, startling a pair of doves into noisy flight. Back in the trees, Gypsy snorted and began to dance nervously. Jessie knew the signs. If she didn't get her mare under control, the skittish creature could bolt and leave her stranded.

Working her knees under her body, Jessie rose to

a crouch. "Settle down, girl," she murmured. "It's all right. We'll soon—"

Her words ended in a scream as the storm-weakened overhang gave way and she plunged into empty space.

Chapter Twelve

Matt heard Jessie's scream as the lip of the overhang broke loose. By the time the massive chunk of earth hit the slope and shattered into pieces, he was already moving, Shouting her name as he galloped his mount wildly up the hill.

"Jessie!" He hadn't seen her fall. Maybe she'd had time to leap to safety as the ledge cracked. He could only pray she hadn't come down with the debris. Nobody could survive such a drop.

"Jessie! Where are you?" He sprang off his horse and clambered up the scree. Fresh boulders and dirt were scattered all around him but he saw no sign of her body.

A sick, cold fear rose in him as he scanned the devastation. Lord, he shouldn't have chased her like this. He should have just let her go. If anything had happened to her, the blame would haunt him to his dying day.

Matt had never been a religious man, but as his eyes searched the broken ledge a hundred feet above him, he prayed. *Please let her be there. Please help me find her. Don't let me lose her before...*

Before what? The question stunned him. What would his future be like if Jessie were gone? He would never hold her again, never kiss her, never battle against her maddeningly strong will. He would never know what she could mean to him.

"Jessie!" He shouted her name at the top of his lungs and heard the echo bouncing off the ledges. Then he heard something else—a terrified whimper that came from somewhere overhead.

His frantic eyes found her at last. She was, perhaps, fifteen feet below the top of the ledge, clinging to a tree root that had been exposed by the breaking overhang. Her hands gripped the twisted surface. Her feet fumbled against the broken cliff face for a purchase that wasn't there.

"Hold on!" He flung himself down the slope and vaulted into the saddle. "I'm coming!"

Still praying, Matt raced the gelding up the narrow deer trail. There was no way to break her fall from below. He would have to get above her and lower the fifty-foot rope he kept coiled on his saddle. If only she could last that long.

He gained the top of the cliff and found the place where the raw earth had broken loose. Enough of the overhang remained to hide her from view. "Jessie, can you hear me?" he shouted, flinging himself out of the saddle.

There was a long, terrible moment of silence. Then her strained answer floated up from below. "Yes…I hear you…can't hold on much longer…"

"I've got a rope." His hands worked as he spoke. "I'm going to lower it down to you. Grab it, you hear?"

Again that awful, heart-stopping silence before her answer. "Yes…hurry!"

He took a precious second to knot the rope's end, making it easier to grip. Then, anchoring a coil around his waist, he tossed the rope over the side of the shattered cliff and waited for the pull of her weight. The rope remained slack.

"What's wrong? Can't you reach it?" His voice rasped with worry.

Silence again. Then a gasp. "No. It's hanging off the ledge—too far out to reach."

Matt stifled a groan. As she fell and grabbed the tree root, her momentum must have swung her beneath what was left of the overhang. There was only one thing he could do.

"I'm coming down," he said.

Pulling up the rope, he kept one end knotted around his waist and tied the other around a sturdy aspen trunk that grew on solid ground a dozen steps back from the edge. A doubled rope would hold their weight more safely but, with the added distance to the aspen, it wouldn't be long enough to reach her. A single length would have to hold them both. The rope was well used and no thicker than his little finger. He could only hope the twisted hemp would be strong enough to preserve Jessie's life as well as his.

Matt gripped the upper part of the rope so that it would play through his hands as he climbed down. Then, flattening onto his belly to distribute his weight, he crawled to the drop-off and lowered himself carefully over the edge. At all costs, he had to avoid causing the fragile overhang that remained to crumble into the canyon, taking Jessie with it.

Scarcely daring to breathe, he inched his way downward. The prickly hemp burned his palms as he slid down the rope, but Matt scarcely felt it. His only thought was for Jessie's safety.

"I see your boots!" she called to him. "Keep coming!"

Matt moved downward as fast as he dared. A few inches, then a few more. Now he could see her hanging from the tree root by her bleeding hands. Beneath the dirt that smeared her skin, her face was chalky white.

"I'm going to swing toward you," he said, inching down to her level. "When I say 'now,' let go and grab me."

Terror flashed in Jessie's eyes. Her lips moved, but no words came out.

"You'll have to trust me, Jessie. Can you do that?"

Pressing her lips together, she nodded. It occurred to Matt that he was asking a lot of her, to trust the man who'd let her brother die. But then, what choice did she have?

Mindful of the crumbling ledge, he shifted his body, twisting the rope and sending it into an easy swing. The first pass wasn't close enough, and he swung outward again. The second pass had more power. "Now!" he shouted as he closed in on her.

In a surge of blind faith, Jessie leaped into space. His free arm caught her waist, jerking her toward him. For a breathless instant her hands clawed at his shirt, then locked around his neck. He had her.

For a moment they dangled in space with the canyon yawning below. Jessie was small and light, but her weight, combined with his, was straining the rope to its limits. If they tried to climb up together, there was a real danger that it might snap. "Can you climb up by yourself?" he asked her.

Trembling against him, she nodded. "My father used to call me his little monkey because I could climb anything."

"Then listen. As soon as you're above me, I'm going to swing in and catch your tree root. It'll take my weight off the rope until you get to the top."

"All right. Here I go." She seized the rope and began to climb. Matt boosted her upward until she was free of him. He could tell she was hurting. She was favoring her left shoulder, and he could see where her scraped hands left traces of blood on the rope, but Jessie neither hesitated nor complained. She was magnificent, he thought.

"Hold on. Here goes!" he called up to her. With the gentlest possible swing he caught the tree root. Releasing his other hand from the rope, which was still knotted around his waist, he hung with his full weight on the twisted root. He could feel the pull in his hands, arms and shoulders. It was a wonder that Jessie had managed to hold on so long.

He couldn't see her now, but the twitching rope told him she was still climbing. The distance was not far, but he knew that every inch would be an ordeal for her.

"Are you all right?" he shouted up to her.

"Yes." Her voice was thin and frightened. "But the ledge—"

A shower of dirt and rocks interrupted her words. Matt's stomach clenched as he realized what she was trying to tell him. The rest of the overhang was starting to crumble away.

"Climb!" he shouted. "Get out of there! Hurry!"

He was waiting to hear she'd made it when the tree root broke loose. Caught off guard, Matt plunged downward a dozen feet before being stopped by the violent jerk of the rope around his waist. For the space of a breath he hung freely, swinging in midair. Then he managed to bend his body, clasp the rope with his hands and pull himself upright.

He could see Jessie now. She was only six or seven feet below the top of the ledge, but she was clearly losing strength. The effort of pulling up was exhausting her. She was moving by mere inches, and now the rope was bearing his full weight as well as hers.

Twisting, she looked down at him. Her eyes were huge and fearful in her small face. "Matt—are you all right?" She spoke with effort.

"Damn it, stop looking and keep climbing!" he rasped. "This rope wasn't made to hold both of us! If you fall, I fall, and I'm not ready to cash in because some lily-livered female didn't have the guts to keep going!"

"Oh, you—" With a grunt of fury, she redoubled her efforts. Matt had calculated that a burst of anger would help get her to the top. His stinging words had hit home.

But there was one more thing he needed to do, and he couldn't let her see it.

Fumbling for the scabbard that hung at his belt, he pulled out a sharp-bladed hunting knife. If the rope weakened and snapped before Jessie reached the top of the cliff, they would both plummet to their deaths. But if he sensed that the strain on the worn hemp was becoming too much he could slice the rope, remove his weight and give her a chance to save herself.

With no family to care for, he had lived his entire twenty-eight years for his own satisfaction—his pride, his profession, his self-serving pleasure. If his death meant that the passionate flame of Jessie's spirit would continue to burn, he would know that his life hadn't been wasted.

"Can you see the rest of the rope?" he called up to her.

"Almost." She grunted with effort, her tone letting him know that she was still angry.

"Don't stand up till you're on solid ground," he warned. "That ledge could give way under your weight."

"I know! Stop lecturing me!" she snapped, twisting her head to glare down at him. The setting sun glinted on the knife blade and he knew from the way her expression froze that she'd seen it and realized what he was prepared to do.

"No, Matt!" she cried. "For the love of heaven, *no!*"

"Climb, damn it!" he snarled up at her. "Just climb!"

Sobbing with effort and emotion, Jessie flung her last ounce of strength into getting to the top of the cliff. She could see over the crumbling edge now. The pressure on the rope was causing it to cut into the surface, sending showers of rocks and dirt over Matt where he hung below her, knife in hand, ready to cut the rope and die for her sake.

She would die with him, Jessie vowed, before she would let that happen.

She had to get off the rope as soon as possible. But the fragile overhang posed an equal danger. Haste, or plain bad luck, could trigger a landslide right down onto Matt's head.

Jessie pulled herself up six more agonizing inches. Now, at last, her head was high enough to see along the full length of the rope to where it was tied around the aspen tree. By now her hands were shredded raw from gripping the rough hemp. Her full weight was still on the rope, but she dared not let go until she could feel solid ground under her feet. For that, she would need to cross the crumbling overhang.

She anxiously scanned the length of the rope, checking for possible weak spots. Her heart froze as she spotted one. It was about halfway between the cliff and the tree, and it was bad. A frayed section as wide as her fist was showing fuzzy ends of broken hemp fibers. How much time would pass before it unraveled and snapped? Minutes? Seconds?

"The rope!" Matt shouted up to her. "Can you see it? Is it holding?"

She thought of his hand gripping the knife, waiting to cut his weight free. "Yes!" she called back. "It's holding fine. Go ahead and start climbing. I'll be up in no time!"

Did he hear the way her voice shook? Did he sense the terror in her lie? Jessie had no time to wonder. She needed to get her weight off the rope before it snapped and sent them both plunging to their deaths.

Hanging on and dragging herself over the top could either break the rope, crumble the overhang or both. There had to be something else she could do.

She frantically searched the cliff and saw a small aspen growing outward from the side, a few feet away. The ground that supported it looked unbroken, but would the thin tree hold her weight? Could she jump far enough to catch it? There was no time to weigh her options. If she didn't make her move now, Matt would die.

Tensing her body, she let go of the rope and flung herself toward the sapling. For an instant she seemed to hang in space. Then her hands caught the base of the thin trunk. Dizzy with fear and relief, she hung there.

"What the hell—?" Matt's voice bellowed up from below.

"Climb!" she screamed. "Hurry! The rope—"

Matt's knife dropped from his hand as he wrenched his body upward. If he didn't make it, she would be lost as well, Jessie realized. There was no way up from where she hung, and neither the tree's thin trunk nor her arms would hold her for long.

In agony, she watched him climb.

Dirt and rocks crashed into the canyon as Matt hauled his body even with the crumbling edge. Now he could see the frayed spot in the rope. He could see the fibers snapping one by one under the strain of his weight. Only a few unbroken strands remained.

Jessie had lied to him about the danger, risking her own life to save his. Now she hung over the void, trusting that he would be strong enough to save them both. He couldn't let her die.

A wordless prayer flashed through his mind as he heaved himself onto the lip of the chasm. He felt the rope part as he rolled, using his momentum to carry him over the crumbling ground. Just short of the tree, he sprang to his feet. He was safe, but the ledge was going down, and he had to get Jessie.

Most of the rope was still tied to his waist. Matt made a rapid circle of the tree to add leverage as he knotted the end and flung it over the cliff. For a sickening moment the worn hemp hung limp. Then relief weakened his knees as it jerked tight.

"Got it!" she shouted. "Pull!"

Bracing his feet against a boulder, Matt hauled her upward, hand over hand. She was featherlight, but the danger of the crumbling edge made every move an exercise in dread. At last he could see her hands, then her dirt-smeared face. Her violet eyes locked with his in unspoken trust.

Sweat trickled down his body as he dragged her up and over the edge. Even under her scant weight, the surface of the ground was beginning to crack.

"Roll toward me fast," he said. "Don't let go, whatever you do."

Her face flashed white in the shadows as her body turned over and over. He caught her as she reached him, jerking her back into the safety of the trees as another six feet of ledge caved in and went crashing down into the canyon.

For a long moment he simply held her in the twilight, feeling her warmth against his pounding heart. She had risked death to save him. That in itself was a small miracle. That they had both survived was almost too much to ask of heaven.

Jessie had begun to tremble. Matt tightened his arms around her, his throat aching. This contrary, argumentative bundle of courage held his heart in her hands. He never wanted to let her go.

His lips brushed her short curls, tasting the damp soil that had fallen on her head. Hellfire, she'd nearly died on that ledge. He wanted to shake her, to scold her, to bully some sense into her. But that would only drive her away, and right now he couldn't stand the thought of having her out of his reach.

The nicker of his horse, waiting behind them in the trees, wrenched him back to reality. "We need to get you home, wherever that is. I don't see your mare."

Jessie stirred, glancing around as she pulled away from him. "Gypsy didn't fall, I'm sure of that. But she likely spooked and bolted when the ledge caved in. She's probably halfway home by now."

"And where's home these days?" Matt would have given anything not to break their fragile truce with words, but he had little choice. "I need to know so I can take you there."

He was braced for an argument, but she only pointed west, toward the peaks. "It's only a few miles. There's a meadow just beyond that first ridge. Years ago an old trapper built a cabin there. We—my family—used to camp there when we went after wild horses."

Matt nodded his understanding and went to get his horse. There were scores of questions in his mind, all shouting to be asked and answered. Why had she run away from him? What had she been doing for the past two weeks? And what kind of craziness had driven her to spy on Virgil and Lillian?

He also needed to tell her about Morgan Tolliver's invitation and persuade her to accept it. But even that could wait until morning. When he tried to talk to Jessie, the words tended to get between them in an irritating way, like a burr under a saddle. Tonight both of them were emotional and exhausted. Trying to talk things out would be a mistake.

And right now the last thing Matt cared about was clearing the air. All he wanted was to be with her.

Riding double, they wound their way up to the ridge. The rising moon, nearly full, flooded the land with pools of light and shadow. Stars glittered like spilled diamonds across the dark expanse of the sky. The night was warm, the breeze a soft caress.

Jessie sat behind Matt on the tall gelding. Her arms clasped his ribs. Her head lay drowsily against his back. He had said no more than a few words to her, and she was glad of it. If he talked, he would lecture her, and if he lectured, she would argue. She was far too exhausted for a fight and so, she sensed, was Matt.

Where her ear lay against his ribs, she could hear the low sound of his breathing and the steady drumming of his heart. His leather vest was smooth and warm against her cheek. When she inhaled, the subtle aromas of wood smoke, fresh hay and clean male sweat drifted into her senses.

Under different conditions, it would have been bliss to simply close her eyes and drift. But there was a war going on inside her—a war between her head and her heart.

The plea of her heart was simple. Matt had nearly

given his life to save her. Surely that meant he cared for her, maybe even loved her. So why shouldn't she feel free to love him in return?

The voice in her mind was more insistent, its argument more complex and compelling. Matt's selfless gesture had nothing to do with love. Frank's loss weighed on his conscience and on his reputation. Another Hammond death would have ruined him, especially when half the county had seen him ride after her. But if, on the other hand, he'd given his life to save her, he would have died a hero. It was honor, not love, that had nearly driven him to cut the rope.

An ambitious man like Matt would want a woman he could be proud of, not the scruffy tomboy sister of an accused murderer—especially when, in his eyes, she could still be a murder suspect herself.

Finding Allister's killer would prove her own innocence, as well as Frank's. But as long as Frank could be blamed, Matt had no reason to help her. If she asked him, he would only tell her to put the tragedy behind her and move on.

Jessie loosened her grip on Matt and forced herself to sit up straight behind him. It was time she put her girlish fantasies aside. Much as she might wish it, Matt Langtry was not going to slay her dragons and fall at her feet. Whatever needed doing, she would have to do on her own.

But right now, all she wanted was to feel his arms around her again.

From the ridge, Matt gazed down at the moonlit meadow where the cabin stood. It was a perfect hideout, sheltered on all sides by rocky peaks. In his search for Jessie, he'd probably passed within a quarter mile of it without realizing it was there.

As the horse shifted to a downhill gait, he felt Jessie stir behind him. She'd fought sleep for most of the past hour but had finally sagged against his back, her fingers locked through his belt loops. Matt had let her doze, savoring the heat of her body through his vest. In the bright moonlight, he hadn't needed her help to find the trail. Unfortunately, in the silence, all his black thoughts had come home to roost.

At least his suspicions about Jessie being the shooter were dwindling. If she'd killed Allister herself, it would have been easy enough to let Frank take the blame. Instead she was risking arrest, or worse, to prove her brother's innocence. Tomorrow he would confront her about her nighttime forays. Tonight he didn't trust himself to speak. He was too vulnerable and so, he sensed, was Jessie.

Behind him, she sat up and stretched, uttering sleepy sounds that made him want to turn around, clasp her in his arms and bury his face between her breasts. For the length of the ride, her nearness had tormented him. Her warmth had seeped into his blood, sending ripples of heat to his loins. He remembered that night in the storm, the feel of her, like slick, wet satin to the touch. He remembered her quivering release against his fingertips and how he had ached for more of her, all of her.

Matt swore under his breath as they neared the cabin. He was tired, sore and so damned horny he could almost taste it. Part of him wanted to stop the horse right here, fling Jessie down in the grass and make love to her. Another part of him wanted to shake her silly for all the grief she'd put him through. In short, he was in a very dangerous mood.

Once again, he would be spending a night alone with her—and this time his self-control was as frayed and fragile as the rope that had held them to the crumbling ledge.

Chapter Thirteen

They found the mare grazing outside the cabin, reins dragging on the ground. Jessie slid off the back of Matt's horse and ran to Gypsy. "You naughty girl!" she scolded, stroking the satiny neck. "I knew you'd be right here, waiting! Shame on you for running off like that!"

The pinto nickered from the makeshift corral off the back of the cabin. Jessie walked over to the aspen log fence and took down the rails that formed the gate. "I should have taken you today," she said, planting a finger-kiss on the old horse's forehead. "At least you wouldn't have run off and left me hanging in midair."

Matt watched her flit from one animal to the other. He knew what she was up to. As long as she was fussing over her horses, she could put off dealing with him. But she had to know she couldn't fuss all night.

There were things that needed settling, and not all of them could wait until morning.

Swinging out of the saddle, he dropped wearily to the ground. "I'll take care of your mare," he said. "Maybe you'd like to go inside and get a fire started."

She hesitated, then spun away and hurried into the cabin. Moments later he saw the faint glow of a candle through the partly open doorway.

As he led the two horses into the corral, Matt surveyed the tiny, windowless shack. The whole structure was no bigger than his room at the boardinghouse. Light flickered through chinks between the rough-hewn logs, and the roof was nothing but moldering sod that looked as if it could collapse under heavy snow. Beyond the corral, he could see a patch of raw earth where Jessie had dug more sod to patch the holes. She had likely taken pains to scrub and repair the inside as well, but at best, her new home was no more than a hovel.

How could she survive in a remote place like this, with no one to help and protect her? Jessie was an accomplished hunter, he knew, but there were wolves, cougars and grizzly bears in these mountains, to say nothing of beasts in human form who lived outside the law. If such men were to come by and find her, he didn't even want to think about what could happen. Even some minor event, such as an illness or an injury, could turn deadly if she were up here alone.

Matt unsaddled the horses and removed their bridles, taking notice of the stream that ran through a corner of the corral. Tomorrow the first order of the day would be to get Jessie out of here. They could talk about what to do next on the ride back to Sheridan.

His nostrils caught the homey fragrance of burning wood. He glanced up to see smoke curling from the blackened tin chimney. The night was getting chilly. He looked forward to the warm cabin and to feasting his eyes on Jessie.

As for the rest—if things got off on the wrong foot, they could both be in for an awkward, miserable night.

As he replaced the aspen rails and walked toward the front door, Matt struggled with what to say to her.

He took a deep breath as he opened the door. What he said and did next, he realized, would have to depend on Jessie.

She glanced up from tending the potbellied stove as he came inside. The single candle, thrust into an old brown bottle on the table, cast a glow that shimmered on her skin, reflecting amber flames in her eyes. Her shorn hair framed her face in childlike tendrils. Even in her ragged flannel shirt and muddy overalls, she was alluringly feminine. His brave, beautiful Jessie. The sight of her made his throat ache.

How could he have wondered what to do, when there was only one answer?

Crossing the distance between them, he laid his

hands on her shoulders and turned her around to face him. The eyes that gazed up at him glimmered with unshed tears.

"Don't touch me," she said huskily. "Not unless it means something."

He gathered her close. For a long breath of time, he simply held her, feeling the frantic pulse of her heart through her rib cage. She trembled against him like a captured bird; fierce little Jessie who was so afraid to trust herself to love.

Lifting her chin with his fingertips, he found her sweet mouth. His kiss was slow and tender. She responded with a low sob that rose from the depths of her body. Her arms slid around his neck, pulling his head down to deepen the contact between them.

Matt felt the heat rise in his body as she pressed against him. He wanted this woman in ways he had no right to want her. But suddenly that right made no difference. She needed him. Filling that need blurred the line between black and white. It made all his long-standing rules seem pompous and silly.

But then, Jessie had never fit the rules. If he made love to her, it couldn't be for a night or even for a few heady weeks. Jessie Hammond was a forever kind of woman, a woman to have and hold and cherish for the rest of his life. If he wasn't ready to offer his heart and hand, it would be better for them both if he walked away right now.

He kissed her again and felt her press against his swollen shaft. Her hips moved, rubbing him through the layers of cloth that kept them chastely apart. Dizzy with the feel of her, he pulled her closer. She gasped, then moaned. He fought for self-control as the spasms rippled through her body. His kisses devoured her eyes, her cheeks her throat as her breathing slowed and she sank against him.

The candle guttered, deepening the shadows around them as they stood wrapped in each other's arms. This was as close as he'd ever come to heaven, Matt thought. He could die a happy man, just holding her.

He would wait for the wedding if that was what she wanted. But Lord, it wasn't going to be easy when Jessie was so responsive and he was so hungry for her. His loins flamed as he imagined taking her here and now, thrusting into her wet, silky darkness, the mounting ecstasy, the rocking explosion as his hot seed filled her.

But he would never hurt Jessie by demanding more than she was ready to give. Whatever he took now would be only what she offered him.

Jessie quivered against him, shaken by the waves of liquid heat that had surged through her body. She had barely tasted what he had to give her, and she wanted the whole, delicious sensual banquet. She wanted to feel his hands stroking her, exploring the places that burned for his touch. She wanted to mold herself to his beautiful, iron-muscled body, to feel his skin gliding over hers as he pushed inside her, deeper, harder, again and again.

She had seen horses breed and felt a contraction in her loins at every powerful thrust of the stallion's massive haunches. As she'd observed the details of the joining, she could not help imagining how it would feel to have that vital part of a man inside her, huge and swollen and eager. She'd found the thought vaguely disturbing, even frightening—until the man had become Matt.

Now, with that hard ridge jutting against her belly, all she could think of was how much she needed him.

Freeing her hand from around his neck, she moved far enough away from him to unhook the straps of her overalls. The baggy garment slid down her body and crumpled around her ankles.

Matt's breath sucked in as he caught her close. One hand slid hungrily upward beneath her shirt and camisole to find her breasts. His palm was rough and raw from gripping the rope. Her nipples puckered as that roughness brushed her tender flesh. Shimmering currents of heat pulsed downward into her legs. She felt a surge of thigh-slicking moisture. She whimpered, ravenous for more. Her eyes closed. Her head fell back.

Tugging her shirt open, he buried his face between her breasts. Her fingers clawed at his hair. Her chest arched upward as she pulled his head closer.

"I want you, Jessie," he muttered, his chapped lips moving against her skin. "Stop me now, if you need to. You might not be able to stop me later."

Jessie's head was swimming. She groped for words. "The…bed…" was all she could manage to say.

The sound he made could have been a chuckle. "Wait, you little wanton…" he muttered.

His hands pulled her shirt and camisole down off her shoulders, leaving her bare above the waist. The feel of him against her bare skin was intoxicating. Frantic for more, she pulled at his shirt, popping a button in her haste. He helped her with the rest, then pulled her against him once more. Jessie's eyes closed as his hands moved over her back. The warm, musky aroma of his body sang in her senses. She inhaled him, tasted the salt on his skin. He groaned as her tongue found one of his nipples, licking and sucking until it hardened. Sweet heaven, how she craved him. She couldn't get enough.

His chest was dusted with a triangle of crisp brown curls. Her exploring fingers traced the narrowing line to where it vanished beneath the belted waist of his trousers. Her pulse lurched to a gallop as she found his belt buckle, unfastened it and began to fumble with the stubborn buttons.

Sensing her frustration, he caught her hand. His eyes twinkled as he pressed his lips into her rope-burned palm. "Allow me," he whispered.

His practiced fingers dispatched the buttons in seconds. "Now, where were we?" he asked, capturing her hand once more. "Tell me what you want to do, Jessie."

"Touch you…love you…" she whispered in a frenzy of need.

He kissed her, his mouth slow and gentle, his tongue coaxing whimpers of pleasure from her throat. Unbidden, her hand slid downward to his waist, then lower to find him. Her fingers clasped the velvet-cloaked hardness of his shaft. A stallion, she thought. Huge and strong and beautiful.

A quiver went through his body as she stroked him. "Yes, the bed…" he whispered, his voice thick and urgent.

She guided him toward the wooden platform that she had cushioned with fresh pine boughs and covered with her quilt. Hastily they shed their boots and what remained of their clothes. The sweet scent of pine rose around them as they tumbled onto the narrow, makeshift bed.

Stretching out, they lay in each other's arms, touching and kissing. His roughened hands caressed her bare skin, awakening every sensitive nerve until her whole body tingled with spasms of desire. Shifting above her, he moved downward to her breasts, kissing her nipples, licking and sucking them until she writhed beneath him. All she could think of was wanting him inside her, thrusting deep into the aching core of her need. "Please, Matt…" she whispered, her hips undulating. "Please…"

Even then he was merciless. Feathering a trail of kisses along her belly, he moved between her parted legs and lowered his head. She gasped at the first brush of his tongue. Then, as waves of exquisite flowering swept through her, she groaned. Her fingers tangled in his hair as she pressed upward against him, almost sobbing in ecstasy.

She was still shuddering when he lunged forward and pushed into her. The long glide carried him deep, causing a prick of pain that vanished in the rush of new sensations, new emotions. She had yearned to be possessed by him; now she was his to the depths of her soul. Instinctively she began to move, meeting his urgent thrusts with her own. Her legs captured him, pulling him deeper, binding his body to hers. Then it was as if she was flying with him, through a shimmering golden fire that flooded every part of her body. The harsh cadence of his breathing matched her own as he shuddered, burst inside her and collapsed in her arms.

For a long moment she held him, overcome by the sweetest love she had ever known. Then, coming back to himself, he stirred, rose up on one elbow and brushed the damp curls back from her face. "Jessie," he whispered. "My dearest Jessie."

Matt awoke to the songs of morning birds and the smell of fresh coffee. His arm fumbled for Jessie. Beside him, the spot on the quilt where she'd slept was empty and cool. Gone. He must have been sleeping like a drunkard not to feel her get up and leave his side.

Jerking himself fully awake, he sat up. His gaze darted around the cabin. The only signs of life were the fire that had burned down to coals in the small iron stove and the coffeepot that simmered on the single burner.

Cursing, he swung his feet to the floor and reached for his trousers. Last night's loving had been heaven on earth. But so help him, if Jessie Hammond had run off again, she was going to be one sorry woman.

Muttering under his breath, he pulled on his clothes and boots and raked a hand through his hair. He could put up with the fact that his mouth felt cottony and his shoulder muscles screamed from hanging on the rope. But the last thing he wanted to deal with was tracking Jessie down again.

The rough plank door was ajar, letting in the first pearlescent rays of sunlight. Striding across the cabin, he yanked it open the rest of the way—and nearly stumbled over Jessie, who was sitting on the stoop drinking coffee from a tin mug.

He stared down at her, feeling foolish for his doubts. She looked fresh and rested, her skin glowing, her curls tousled by the morning breeze. She'd abandoned her overalls for a clean plaid shirt and denim trousers, cinched to her minuscule waist by a wide belt. The awareness that this beautiful creature had spent the night in his arms made him weak in the knees.

Matt cleared his throat to speak, but she put a cautioning finger to her lips. "Look," she whispered, nodding toward the meadow.

Dropping to a crouch beside her, he followed the direction of her focus. Through the long grass, his eyes made out the shape of a wild mustang, then another and another, mares and foals and yearlings, drifting like ghosts in the paleness of dawn. The black stallion moved among them like a living shadow, darting here and there, nudging and nipping as he rounded up his herd.

Matt's hand eased onto Jessie's shoulder, fingers tightening as they shared the morning stillness and the magic of the wild horses. God willing, they would share many such moments in years to come, and countless nights of loving as well. But the issues they'd put aside last night couldn't wait any longer. It was time for some serious talk.

In the corral behind the cabin, Jessie's mare and

the two geldings were becoming agitated. Matt could hear them snorting and banging their bodies against the fragile fence. Unless they were calmed, they might knock down the rails to mingle with the wild mustangs.

He rose to his feet. Seeing the movement, the stallion gave a whistle of alarm. Instantly the mustangs wheeled and thundered away toward higher ground, leaving only the sigh of wind in the long spring grass.

Matt went around to the rear of the cabin to quiet the three horses, take care of his needs and splash his face and hands with water from the creek. When he returned a few minutes later, Jessie was sitting where he'd left her, balancing the tin mug between her hands.

"Have some coffee," she said. "I only have one cup, but I just refilled it for you. Careful, it's hot."

Matt settled himself beside her and accepted the coffee. The first sip steamed down his throat, black and rich and bracing. If he hadn't been fully awake before, he was now.

How tempting it would be, he thought, to wrap her in his arms and hold her in stillness as the sun rose over the mountains, then sweep her back to the bed for more glorious loving. But there were things that needed to be said, things that had already waited too long. He took another sip of the scalding coffee, his mind groping for the best way to begin.

It was Jessie who broke the silence. "Yesterday

you said you had good news for me. Does that mean you know who killed Allister?"

She watched him guardedly. He should have known she'd be ready for him, and that she would be as direct as a gunshot to the heart.

He shook his head. "Not yet. But I spoke with Morgan Tolliver at the funeral. He believes that Frank was innocent, and he's offered you a place on his ranch, for as long as you want to stay. He said he could use someone who's good with horses. I've come to take you there. We can leave as soon as you're ready."

The hurt that stole across her face warned Matt that he'd already said the wrong thing. Last night he had made passionate love to her. Now, as she likely saw it, he was planning to dump her with the Tollivers and be done with her.

"It wouldn't be for long," he said, capturing her hand in his. "Just until we get things sorted out and I can find us a place to live. I want to marry you, Jessie, as soon as the time's right."

"You needn't be so noble." She snatched her hand away. "Whatever your precious honor demands, I'm not asking you to make an honest woman of me. As for the Tollivers, please give them my thanks, but I won't burden them with my troubles. I'll be fine right here, on my own!"

Matt swallowed a string of curses as his frustration began to boil. Blast the woman, she was doing it again—turning him into a fuming, seething wild man. The fact that he loved her so much, and that he was so concerned for her safety, only made things worse.

The cup clattered to the ground, spilling a stream of coffee as he seized her shoulders. "Listen to me, Jessie," he said, gripping her firmly. "You can't stay here, damn it. It isn't safe. And you've got to stop those crazy nighttime forays onto the Gates Ranch. Sooner or later you're going to get caught!"

"Oh?" Her eyes blazed defiance. "And who's going to clear my brother's name if I give up trying? I could get old and gray waiting for you to do the job, Matt Langtry!"

"That's not fair. I've searched for evidence, talked to witnesses, done everything I could, within the limits of the law—"

"Hang the law!" She twisted free of his grip. "Did you know Lillian and Virgil were lovers?"

"I guessed as much from watching them. And I didn't have to peek in any bedroom windows to do that."

"Well?" She stared at him expectantly.

"Adultery and murder are two different things, Jessie. I can hardly arrest them for sleeping together."

"For heaven's sake, don't you see?" She seized his wrist, her voice rough with urgency. "If Virgil had fallen in love with his brother's wife, that would have given him the perfect motive to kill Allister. He'd not only be getting Lillian, he'd be getting Allister's half of the ranch as well! The shooter had to be Virgil!"

Matt sighed wearily. "There's one flaw in your argument. Virgil was playing cards in town when Allister was shot. The old man who tends bar at Smitty's backed up his story. Virgil was there until eleven. By the time he got home, Allister was already dead."

Jessie looked crestfallen. "But he could have paid the old bartender to say that. Or he could have hired one of his men to kill Allister while he was away."

"Think about it. Nobody knew Frank was going to be at the ranch, or that Allister would come outside and catch him taking the stallion. And nobody knew that Frank was going to drop his rifle and leave it behind. Unless your brother shot Allister, the murder was a crime of opportunity. Anyone who happened along could have pulled that trigger."

"Or anyone who was watching, waiting to see what would happen." Her face paled. "You still think it could have been me, don't you?"

Matt leaned back against the door frame, stretching his legs in the warming sunlight. "No," he said, watching her through slitted eyes. "You don't have it in you to kill a man, Jessie, or to lie about it if you had. Everything you've told me about that night rings true."

"Including the part about not hearing a shot? Does that mean you believe Frank was innocent?" Her eyes pleaded for understanding. He could not help re-membering those eyes gazing up at him in the can-dlelight as he made love to her.

"I believe it," Matt said, weighing his words. "But that doesn't mean I can prove it to anyone else. There's no evidence—"

"There has to be evidence! If we keep looking, surely we'll find it!"

"Not *we,* Jessie." Matt scowled at her, knowing he had to make her listen. "You're to stay out of this and leave the detective work to me. No more snooping around the Gates Ranch, or anywhere else. It's too dangerous. Do you understand?"

She glowered at him, saying nothing.

"Trust me, Jessie, that's all I'm asking. I want the truth as much as you do. But I need to find it in a way that won't break the law."

She broke eye contact and looked down at her hands, still refusing to answer.

"Come on, let's have a bite to eat, and then I'll help you pack," he said, rising to his feet. "We'll have plenty of time to talk about this on the way down the mountain."

"No."

"No?" He stared at her, caught off guard.

"I told you, I'm staying here. I'll be fine."

"Blast it, Jessie, listen to me!" he exploded, ris-ing to his feet.

"No, you listen to me, Matt Langtry." She was on her feet also, her voice so tightly controlled that he could see the strained cords in her neck. "Last night was wonderful. I can't fault you for taking what I was willing to give. But I'm not exactly the sort of woman you'd want on your arm in public, am I?"

"What the devil are you talking about?"

"Your rules, your honor, your precious reputation—it's as if you need to prove that you're better than ordinary people. Maybe it's because of the way you were raised, without knowing who your father was. Maybe it's something I'm not even aware of. But you'd never take a public stand against the likes of Virgil Gates for the sake of a poor, innocent mountain boy who died in your custody. And you wouldn't be caught dead walking down Main Street in Sheridan with that boy's sister!"

Matt felt the color drain from his face as her words sank home. "You're wrong, Jessie. And this conversation isn't about me. It's about getting you to the Tollivers, where you'll be safe."

"I'm safe enough here. If I need to, I can get to the Tolliver Ranch by myself."

"I could arrest you and take you in. You'd be safe in jail."

"Arrest me? For what?" She showed no sign of fear.

"Trespassing, arson, assaulting a federal officer. Take your pick."

"You wouldn't dare!" Her blazing eyes challenged him.

"Wouldn't I?" He took a step toward her. His words had been no more than an empty threat, but Jessie's eyes widened in sudden fear.

Losing her nerve, she spun away with a little gasp and bolted into the cabin, slamming the door behind her.

Matt swore as he heard the bolt slide into place. Last night, with Jessie in his arms, the future had seemed clear and fine. Now his whole world had turned upside down, and he didn't know how to set it right.

Trying to coax her outside, he knew, would only add fuel to the fire. Jessie needed time to sort things out. Maybe once she did, she would realize that he loved her and was only trying to protect her. But meanwhile, all he could do was leave her alone.

Feeling as if he'd been gut-kicked, Matt strode around to the corral and saddled his horse. As soon as he got back to Sheridan, he would send a message to Morgan Tolliver, telling him where Jessie was and urging him to bring her down to the ranch. Hopefully Morgan would be able to talk some sense into the stubborn little fool. Matt could only wish he'd been able to do it himself.

Had Jessie been right about him? Was he so hungry for acceptance that he couldn't step out of line, even for the right reason? Was it his lack of a father that had driven him to make something of himself at the expense of love and compassion? Was that why he'd never let anyone close to him?

Her words had shaken him to the core. In the hours ahead, he would turn those words over in his mind and try his best to understand them. If he failed, he knew that Jessie would be lost to him forever.

Easing his sore body into the saddle, he rode around to the front of the house. The door was tightly closed, as he'd known it would be.

Almost as an afterthought, he took the leather pouch, containing the fifty-dollar prize, out of his vest pocket and tossed it onto the stoop. Then he wheeled his horse and rode down the mountain.

Chapter Fourteen

What had she done?

Jessie slumped on the edge of the bed, her hands clasped between her knees, as the sound of Matt's galloping horse faded into silence.

Part of her wanted to rush outside, bridle her mare and race after him, shouting that she'd rather go to jail than live without him. But she'd already made a complete fool of herself. Why worsen the melodrama by begging?

Would Matt really have arrested her? Probably not. But she'd frustrated him to the point where he'd washed his hands of her. He wouldn't be coming back. Not if he had a lick of sense.

Morning sunlight streamed through the chinks between the logs, falling in bright patterns on the quilt where she and Matt had made love. As Jessie rose to her feet, the raw twinge between her legs reminded her that her innocence was gone forever. She had flung it away in love and joy and had no regrets—not even now.

Last night, for a time, she'd let herself believe he loved her, too. But his callous, offhand proposal—if it could even be called that—had shown her the truth. If she still wanted him, after spending time with the Tollivers, he would be willing to do his duty.

Duty. What a miserable, heartbreaking word, she thought. And it was the very word that ruled Matt Langtry's life. Where were his emotions—did he even have any? Where was his heart—would he ever listen to its call? Or would his days be one long march to the grinding cadence of duty…duty…duty…?

Why couldn't he have told her he loved her? Maybe that would have made the difference.

Opening the door, she walked outside. The sunlight was blinding after the dim interior of the cabin. In its glare, she thought she saw a rider emerging over the crest of the trail. Her heart gave a glorious bound then plummeted as her vision cleared. She was staring at a twisted stump on the far side of the meadow.

Her foot touched the leather pouch on the stoop. Fighting the temptation to throw it into the trees, she picked it up and shoved it into her pocket. The prize money was rightfully Matt's, not hers. If she ever saw him again, she'd pay it back—with interest.

But she'd brooded about Matt long enough, Jessie told herself, sinking onto the stoop. It was time to return to her own duty and clear her brother's name once and for all.

She'd come up with scattered bits of information, and Matt had given her still more. If she put everything together, like the pieces of a puzzle, maybe the emerging picture would show her something new.

Smoothing the dirt at her feet, she found a sharp twig and began to sketch out a map of the Gates Ranch and the surrounding land. She drew in Goose Creek, the fences, the roads, the house, the corral, the barn and the other outbuildings, even the trees and brush. Then she extended the roads and trails in the direction of town.

Now she needed people.

Walking around to the corral, she reached into the streambed, scraped up a handful of water-tumbled pebbles and carried them back to her map. The largest one, brown and slightly rough, she designated as Virgil. A smooth, gray stone was Allister, a dark, narrow one Frank. Her own pebble was small and golden, Lillian's brightly polished and dark green in color. The rest of the pebbles were used to represent the hired help—house servants and ranch hands.

She placed her own pebble first, on the far side of the creek where she'd waited for Frank with the mare. Virgil's was placed off the map, in the area she'd designated as the town. After a moment's thought, she laid Frank's stone next to her own, by the creek. Since Allister and Lillian had been man and wife, she placed theirs in the house, close together, likely in the same bedroom.

The ranch hands would have been asleep in the bunkhouse, although she could not be certain of that. Likewise, the servants would have retired to their quarters behind the main house. She scattered the remaining pebbles in both locations.

As she studied her map, Jessie soon realized that she couldn't account for the movements of everyone on the ranch. She could only start with what she knew firsthand, and go on from there.

Picking up the narrow stone that represented Frank, she moved it along the road, through the gate and into the corral, which sided on the barn where Midnight had been stabled. Frank had gone into the barn, freed the stallion and was leading him out of barn when Allister, who'd emerged from the house with his pistol, had met him at the gate of the corral.

Weighing the possibilities, Jessie moved Frank's stone out of the barn. At the same time, she moved Allister's stone out of the house, putting them together at the corral gate. Then she sat back to study the picture she'd made.

It had been a little after ten o'clock when she and Frank had arrived at the creek, and he'd gone in on foot to get the stallion. According to Frank, the house had been dark when he arrived, so Allister and his wife would have been in bed—but not asleep, perhaps. Otherwise, Allister wouldn't have heard the horses and known something was amiss.

Virgil had been in town at that hour and, although she was loath to set the odious man aside as a suspect, Matt had been right about one thing. There was no way Virgil could have known what was going to happen. Reluctantly, she left the brown pebble in place.

The bunkhouse and the servants' quarters lay beyond the house, a good fifty yards from the corral. Unless Allister and Frank had been shouting at the tops of their lungs, it would have been difficult to rouse anyone sleeping inside.

True, Jessie reasoned, one of the hands, or even one of the servants, could have been prowling outside in the darkness. But why? And what was the chance they'd have wanted to kill their employer? It was a possible explanation, but not a likely one.

As Jessie stared down at her puzzle, the last piece slipped into place. The hair rose on the back of her neck as she realized there was only one person who could have killed Allister Gates, and she knew, with gut-clenching certainty, who it was.

Now all she needed was a way to prove it.

By the time Matt arrived back in Sheridan, the sun was approaching the peak of the sky. His empty belly was growling with hunger, but before he took the time to eat, there were three tasks he'd resolved to carry out.

The first was to visit the telegraph office to see if word had come back from St. Louis regarding Lillian's history. Finding that nothing had arrived, he scribbled a terse second request, sent it off and told the operator he would check back later that afternoon.

He used the pen and paper at the telegraph office to write a note to Morgan. On the back of the note he drew a map showing the location of Jessie's cabin. He told Morgan that she appeared safe for now, but if he didn't hear from her in the next few days, he might want to ride up there, or send someone she'd recognize, and bring her down to the ranch.

At the livery stable he found a willing youth and paid him to carry the note to the Tolliver Ranch. Finally, returning to his own office, he sat down to begin the third task.

He had pondered Jessie's angry accusations all the way back to town. Much as it stung to admit it, there was truth in what she'd said. For all of his adult life, he'd been driven by the need to belong, to fit in and be looked up to by others. That need had compelled him to follow a strict code of rules—not necessarily what was right, but what would make him accepted. It had guided his decision to become a lawman. And finally, it had driven him to seek out one of the most respected families in the territory and to claim them—privately, at least—as his kin.

Only today, seared by Jessie's impassioned words, had he stopped to count the cost.

Who was Matthew Tolliver Langtry? He was a man who defined himself by other people's expectations, who weighed every consequence, thought before he acted and prided himself on keeping his true feelings under lock and key.

He was a man who had everything to learn from a beautiful little spitfire whose passion for truth, justice, loyalty and unconditional love burned like a rainbow flame. Warm, impulsive, tender Jessie was his salvation, his best and brightest hope. He could not bear to live another day without her.

Tonight, by heaven, he was going to ride back up to that cabin, fall at her feet and beg her to be his. But right now he had a letter to write, one that needed to be written before he could move on with his life.

For a moment Matt stared down at the blank paper. Then he dipped his pen into the inkwell and began to write.

Mr. Hamilton Crawford
118 Kearny Street
Laramie, Wyoming

Dear Mr. Crawford:
Two months ago I paid you a retainer to investigate the history of Jacob Tolliver, specifically

whether Mr. Tolliver had been in Texas nine months before the date of my birth, under circumstances in which he might have known my mother, Sally Langtry.

I no longer wish to know whether Mr. Tolliver was my father. Please terminate your investigation, destroy any information you have on Mr. Tolliver, and send me a bill for your services. Thank you. I appreciate your efforts on my behalf.

Respectfully yours,

Matthew T. Langtry, U.S. Deputy Marshal

Matt folded and addressed the letter and carried it to the post office in time for the afternoon stage. He felt a curious lightness as he walked away. He had never known his own father. But his children would know theirs. He would be there to provide for them, to guide, teach and protect them. And he would love their mother to the end of his days. That was all that mattered.

Being a lawman was dangerous, demanding work. It required a man to be away from home for days, even weeks at a time. He wouldn't want that for his family. He would want to be there whenever they needed him.

Matt had saved much of his income over the years,

and the money had earned a good rate of interest. By now, he calculated, there ought to be enough in the account to buy the small ranch he'd dreamed of owning one day. Maybe it was time to make that dream come true—with Jessie.

By the time Matt had eaten and taken care of some urgent paperwork, it was late afternoon. It would be well after dark when he arrived at Jessie's cabin, but that shouldn't matter. He knew the trail, and there would be a full moon to light his way. He could only pray that she would hear him out and return with him. If she refused… A cold needle of doubt jabbed Matt's heart. Jessie had turned him down once. What if he couldn't change her mind?

That was why he'd contacted Morgan, Matt reminded himself. At least, if something went wrong, there'd be someone else who knew where Jessie was and could get her to safety.

Either way, one thing was certain—Jessie would not be ready to move on with her life until the issue of her brother's murder charge was laid to rest. She had taken on a personal vendetta. Until she made her peace with the past, he could not add to her burden by asking her to be his wife.

And Matt had his own reasons for wanting to find Allister's killer. Because of that crime, a young man had suffered a tragic, needless death. Frank Hammond deserved justice. Matt couldn't think of his own future until that justice was done. He owed the boy that much.

He had picked up Copper at the livery stable and was headed out of town when he remembered that he hadn't checked back at the telegraph office. For a moment Matt was tempted to keep riding. He'd grown frustrated waiting for word from St. Louis, and he was anxious to get to Jessie.

He hesitated, then sighed and turned the big gelding back toward town. Experience had taught him to follow through on every detail. If he left without checking for a message, he would always wonder if it might have made a difference.

The telegraph operator was just locking up for the day. As Matt swung off his horse, the wiry, bespectacled man waved the envelope in his hand. "This just came for you, Marshal," he said. "I was going to leave it at your office on my way home."

Thanking him, Matt ripped open the envelope and yanked out the message inside. As his fingers unfolded the paper, he braced himself for disappointing news. Not all his hunches paid off. For all he knew, Lillian Gates could be as saintly as she was beautiful.

But as he stared down at the printed letters, he knew that wasn't the case. His hunch had been dead-on.

Stuffing the telegram into his pocket, Matt sprang into the saddle and jabbed his boots into Copper's flanks. He had no evidence to prove that Lillian had murdered her husband, but sooner or later he would find it. Meanwhile, he needed to get to Jessie before she took another crazy chance. She was dealing with a black widow. One more misadventure could trap her in a deadly web, with no way out.

Several hours later, Matt paused on the ridge above the cabin to rest his lathered horse. He had pushed the big chestnut as hard as he dared, all the way up the meandering trail. Even so, the setting sun had won the race. The mountains lay cloaked in deep twilight, brightened above the peaks by the platinum rim of the moon.

With every mile he rode, Matt's fear for Jessie had grown. When he reached the cabin, he saw there was no light flickering between the logs, no smoke drifting out of the chimney. Matt cursed in desperation. Damn it, he should have known she'd take off on her own. Why hadn't he stayed with her—or better yet, broken down the door, flung her over his shoulder and hauled her down the mountain?

As he rode up to the cabin, hope still burned that she might have taken refuge with the Tollivers. But the nicker of the spotted packhorse from the corral laid that idea to rest. If she'd gone to the Tolliver Ranch, she would have taken both horses. The pinto's presence was a sure sign that Jessie had meant to return, which could only mean one thing.

Jessie was in danger, and he had to go after her.

Slipping off the mare's back, Jessie looped the bridle around a willow that grew beside the water. On her previous two visits to the Gates Ranch, she'd ridden Spade and left him in the hills outside town. This time, fearing the need to make a fast getaway, she'd decided to take Gypsy and leave her at the creek, where she'd waited for Frank on the night of Allister's death.

She had pondered long and hard about how to prove that Lillian had killed her husband. The woman's affair with Virgil lent motive but little else. As for evidence, any that might have existed had been trampled into the ground. Only a confession, or the word of someone who knew, would tie Allister's glamorous widow to his murder.

Jessie knew she'd be running a terrible risk. But desperate times called for desperate measures. When a rat wouldn't come out of its hole, you put out bait and waited for the creature to make a move. That's what she'd be doing tonight. But she would have to be excruciatingly careful. She was dealing with a very dangerous rat.

Emerging from the willows, she crouched at the edge of the road. From here she could see the house with its ornate portico, ghostly under a fresh coat of whitewash. Light gleamed from the parlor windows. There was no sign of movement in the yard. Her timing, Jessie calculated, was about right.

As she rose to her feet, the folded note crackled in her pocket. She had written it on an end paper from one of her precious books, using a pencil stub she'd found in the cabin. The words, printed in crude block letters, had burned themselves into her memory.

> I know you killed your husband, Lillian.
> Meet me at his grave, 11 tonight. Come alone.

The thought of what she was about to do turned the blood in her veins to cold jelly. She yearned for Matt's quiet strength beside her. But Matt would have called her scheme crazy and done everything in his power to stop her. He would have insisted on keeping everything legal and above board—and Frank would go down in history as the murderer of Allister Gates. This was the only way to clear his name.

Would Lillian come to the cemetery? How could she not come? She would be too frightened, angry and curious to stay away.

The woman would surely bring a gun. And Virgil would likely be nearby, lurking in the shadows. But Jessie had no plans to confront them. She would simply watch and listen from a safe hiding place. If Lillian even showed up, it would be damning enough. If she shouted threats into the darkness, offered money or conversed with Virgil about what she'd done, it would be—as Jessie's mother might have put it—frosting on the cake.

Tomorrow, if all went as planned, she would ride into Sheridan, find Matt and tell him what she'd learned. He would be furious with her, Jessie knew. But in the end he would have to believe her and take action to find more proof against Lillian.

And if he didn't? Doubts gnawed at her mind as she crept toward the house. She forced them away. For all his irritating ways, Matt was a good man. She could trust him to keep her safe and to do the right thing.

But could Matt trust her? Jessie felt her knees weaken as the memories struck her like an autumn storm—Matt with his knife in his hand, ready to cut the breaking rope and save her life; Matt bending over her in the candlelight, his love carrying her to heaven and back. He had given her a taste of what they could have together. It could be hers—if only she abandoned this headstrong quest to clear Frank's name.

Matt had asked for her trust. Going ahead with this plan would be a betrayal of that trust. He might accept her evidence and use it to arrest Lillian. But the fragile bond between them would be broken, never to heal.

Torn, she stumbled into the shadow of the barn

and sank to the ground. It wasn't too late, she told herself. She could turn back now, find Matt in Sheridan and patch up their differences. A lifetime of love was waiting. All she had to do was stop right here, walk back to her mare and ride away.

Jessie pressed her hands to her face, struggling to clear her thoughts. No, she realized, she had to see this through.

Pulling herself to her feet, she crept on toward the house. Lamps still burned in the parlor, but nowhere else in the house. It stood to reason that the servants had finished their work and retired to their own quarters, leaving Virgil and Lillian alone.

The night was cool, but as she neared the new cement steps that led up to the portico, nervous sweat trickled down her body. So far everything had gone well. Too well, perhaps. Nothing seemed amiss, but she could not shake the feeling that something was wrong.

At the foot of the steps, she reached into her trousers for the note. Her hand was still in her pocket when she heard a low, menacing growl. The sound had barely registered before a huge black dog came charging around the corner of the house. Moonlight glinted on long, yellow fangs as it sprang for her.

There was no time to run. Instinctively, Jessie's hands went up to shield her face and throat. She felt the hot, wet breath, smelled the foulness as the massive weight struck her, knocking her to the gravel. Twisting desperately, she managed to roll onto her belly, but there was nothing she could do to protect her legs and back.

The awful fangs ripped through her trouser leg. Jessie felt them sink into her calf as the door opened, flooding the portico with light.

Chapter Fifteen

⟨ornament⟩

"Who's out there?" The voice was Virgil's. Jessie heard the scrape of his boots on the concrete steps, then the thud of a heavy object striking flesh and bone. The dog yelped, releasing its grip on her leg. Another blow sent it whimpering around the corner of the house.

Dropping the heavy iron bar he'd held, Virgil reached down and yanked Jessie to her feet. Lantern light glinted on his big, horsey teeth as he grinned down at her.

"I'll be damned, if it isn't another Hammond! The sister this time! That ugly mutt was worth every cent I paid for him!"

Jessie glared up at him in silence. She could feel the blood trickling down her leg and into her boot. But that was the least of her problems now.

Virgil's clasp tightened on her arm, bruising her

flesh. "You've been here before, haven't you, girlie? Sneaking around the house, looking in the windows. Care to tell me what you're up to before I break your arm and throw you back to the dog?"

Jessie groped for an excuse that would mollify the man, but he had her dead to rights. There wasn't a lie on earth that would save her. The only weapon she could use against him was the truth.

"Well?" He twisted her arm, making her gasp with pain.

"I…came to see Lil—Mrs. Gates." Jessie spoke through clenched teeth. "Need to ask her something…"

"Ask her what?" He shifted the angle of her arm, increasing the pressure on her shoulder joint. Jessie's knees buckled from the pain. She'd begun to feel nauseous. Virgil was enjoying this, she realized. It made little difference whether she told him anything or not.

"Please…" she whimpered. "Take me inside. Let me talk to her."

"About what?" he demanded again. "Any business of Lillian's is my business."

"About my…brother. You'll want to hear this, too." A wave of dizziness swept over. She was going to pass out, Jessie thought. But her words had caught his interest. Abruptly he loosened his grip. Caught off guard, she crumpled to her knees.

"Come on!" Seizing her other arm, he yanked her

to her feet and up the steps. She stumbled after him, her left boot soggy with blood.

They passed through the entry hall, with its towering grandfather clock, and into the parlor. Hurt and frightened as she was, Jessie could not help being struck by the grandeur of the room, with its crystal chandelier, velvet furnishings and creamy, gold-patterned carpet. But all other thoughts vanished at the sight of the woman who rose from the settee—a woman whose beautiful face exuded a cold evil.

"Did you search her?" Lillian demanded.

When Virgil shook his head, she frowned. "You should have done that before you brought her in here. The little witch could have a gun or a knife on her."

"I'm not armed. You can see that." Jessie was still dressed in the close-fitting shirt and trousers she'd put on that morning. Even a small weapon would have made a visible bulge beneath her clothes.

Lillian's cold eyes looked her up and down. "There's something in your right pocket. Empty both your pockets, Miss Hammond. No tricks. Then you can tell me what you've been doing on our property."

Jessie reached into her pocket and pulled out the leather pouch containing the coins from the race. Virgil took it from her, hefted it in one hand and, at a stern glance from Lillian, laid it on a side table.

"That's all?" Lillian asked, one eyebrow sliding upward. "Turn your pockets inside out. I want to make sure you're not hiding anything."

Jessie pulled out the lining of the left pocket, which was empty. Her right pocket still held the note. For an instant she considered trying to hide it. But no, they would likely kill her in any case. If she was going to die, she would do it with the truth on her lips.

Meeting Lillian's feral gaze, she reached into her right pocket and slowly pulled out the lining. The note dropped to the carpet. Lillian glanced at Virgil, who bent over and picked it up. Unbidden, he unfolded the paper and read what Jessie had written.

Watching him, Jessie saw the blood drain from his face. Her heart lurched as she realized what was happening. *Virgil hadn't known!* Until now, he'd believed it was Frank who'd killed his brother. The truth had hit him like a shot of cold lead, straight through the heart.

"Well, what does it say?" Lillian snapped impatiently. "If the cat's got your tongue, then give it to me! I'll read it myself!"

She took the paper from his rigid hand. Jessie saw her pale beneath her rouge as she read it, but she recovered her poise, crumpled the note and tossed it to the floor. "Rubbish!" she exclaimed. "The girl's delusional, or she wants money! Frank Hammond killed my husband, we all know that!"

"No." Jessie spoke up boldly, knowing the words might be her last. "I was waiting for Frank by the creek that night. He told me what happened. Allister made him drop the rifle. Then the stallion reared, knocking Allister down. Frank jumped on the horse and got away, but he was so scared that he left his rifle behind."

"No!" Lillian's eyes swung from Jessie to Virgil, who appeared to be in shock. "She's lying! It was that horrid boy who shot Allister! I know—I followed Allister outside that night. I was watching. I saw him do it!"

"You saw Frank leave the rifle," Jessie said calmly. "As he rode away you saw your chance. You came out to the corral, picked up the gun and used it to make yourself a rich widow."

"You little liar!" Lillian's hand flashed out, striking Jessie's face. Jessie stood like stone, her gaze unflinching.

"You know she's lying, don't you, Virgil?" Lillian's voice betrayed a thread of fear as she reached out and clasped Virgil's arm. "Tell me you believe me, dearest!"

He stared down at her white hand, where it lay on his dark sleeve. "You told me—and told the marshal—that you were in the house when you heard the shot. You never said you followed Allister outside. Not until now. So who's lying? You tell me."

She turned on him, suddenly wild. "You promised me you'd do it! That first night in your room, you said you'd kill him for me. But you didn't have the guts, did you? I waited and waited. Finally I saw the perfect chance, and I took it! I did it for us, Virgil! For you and me!"

Virgil stared down at her, his mouth twisting with emotion. "I'd have promised anything to get you in my bed, Lil," he said. "But murder my own brother? Lord, woman, I've done some bad things in my time, but I could never do that! When he got shot, and it looked like the Hammond kid did it, I figured maybe that was how things were meant to be."

"It was! It is!" Lillian flung her arms around him as Jessie, almost forgotten now, edged toward the door. "We can have a fine life now, everything we ever wanted—"

He pulled away from her. "I've got to give this some thought, Lil."

She seized the front of his shirt, her eyes savage now. "So help me, Virgil, if you turn against me now, I'll take you down with me! I'll say you were in on Allister's murder, that we planned it together—"

Jessie didn't wait to hear more. She was out of the parlor, racing through the entry hall, out the front door and onto the portico. Her leg was still bleeding, but her fear was stronger than her pain. She ran full out.

The iron bar Virgil had dropped lay at the foot of

the steps. Remembering the dog, Jessie snatched it up and kept on running. As she reached the corral fence, she heard the scream of a woman's voice. The sound faltered, broke and ended in blood-chilling silence.

Jessie had just passed the barn when she heard the dog. It was coming fast behind her, panting and snarling. Knowing she couldn't outrun the creature, she raised the bar and turned, braced to meet the flashing fangs.

But the sight of the bar was enough. As Jessie held it up, her arm poised to strike, the dog turned tail and slunk back toward the house. Weak with relief, Jessie gathered her strength for the final sprint to the creek. Virgil would be coming after her as soon as he could mount his big piebald horse. After what she'd seen and heard, Jessie knew he could not afford to let her get away.

Glancing toward the house, she saw a dancing light in the parlor window. But there was no time to wonder what was happening or to think about the scream she'd heard. She had to get to her mare and get away from here.

She could feel the spongy wetness in her boot as she ran, but there was no pain. When she got to a safe place, she would stop and wrap her leg. Until then it would just have to bleed.

A dry wind had sprung up, rippling the long pasture grass like waves on a waterless sea. Ahead in the moonlight she could see the willows that edged the creek. Gypsy snorted nervously at her approach, as if sensing terror in the air. Jessie untied the mare and flung herself into the saddle. As they turned toward the main road, some half-heard sound made her look back toward the house.

Flames were shooting out of the lower windows, rising as high as the roof.

By the time she passed the cemetery, Jessie knew she was being followed. Pausing to listen behind her, she heard, above the pounding of her heart, not one set of hoofbeats, but two. Virgil, she calculated, must have stayed behind and sent his hired guns after her. They would have orders to make sure she didn't live to tell what she knew.

And what did she know? As the mare flew along the moonlit road, she tried to piece together what had happened. Before Jessie had escaped, she'd heard Lillian confess to shooting Allister and threaten to implicate Virgil if he turned her in. After that, judging from the scream, Virgil could have attacked the woman, maybe strangled or stabbed her, then set the house on fire to cover his crime. Or maybe they'd struggled, knocking over a kerosene lamp and setting the room ablaze.

A sickening fear curdled Jessie's stomach as she realized what she'd set in motion tonight. It didn't make any difference whether she lived or died. She'd been at the ranch. Her tracks were on the ground. Assuming he survived the fire, Virgil would blame her for setting fire to the house—and he would be believed. Why not? It was no secret that she hated the Gates family, or that she'd burned her own ranch before Virgil took possession of the place. Who wouldn't believe him?

Even Matt?

Her pursuers were still behind her, holding their own, maybe even gaining. This time there was no chance of losing them in the mountains.

Less than a mile ahead, a wagon trail branched off the main road and cut north toward the Tolliver Ranch. Jessie hadn't wanted to involve the Tollivers in her problems but now she had no choice.

Hunching over Gypsy's neck, Jessie dug in her heels and shot northward across the prairie.

Matt emerged from the trees below the burned-out Hammond place. Here, where the trail followed the open ridge, he could look out over the valley below.

What he saw stopped his heart.

Beyond Felton, where the land dropped down toward Goose Creek, a crimson glow blazed and flickered, spreading like a bloody wound against the dark night sky.

Fire. And the flames appeared to be coming from the Gates Ranch.

Even at a frantic pace, it took him half an hour to descend the steep trail. By the time Matt thundered down the wagon road and into the town, the streets of Felton were swarming with activity. Men, women and children were outside staring at the fiery sky as if the Second Coming were at hand.

"What's going on?" He stopped a bearded man carrying several empty buckets.

"Fire at the Gates place! I hear the house is too far gone to save, but we're goin' out to help. In this wind…" He looked up at the sky and shook his head. "Maybe we can at least keep it from spreadin' to the prairie."

"Does anybody know how it started?"

"I heard tell it was the Hammond girl. Makes sense, bein' she burned down her own place afore Virgil took it over."

Matt had already known what he would hear. Still, he felt as if his heart were sinking into his stomach. All his instincts told him Jessie was innocent. True, she was rash and impulsive, but she was no fool. She would have known that she was sure to be blamed for such an act.

And the person who'd set the fire would have known it, too.

Steering his horse through the crowd, Matt made for the road that cut out of town to the Gates Ranch.

As he forded the shallow creek and emerged from

the willows, he had a clear view of the blazing house. It appeared that the fire had started on the ground floor. The lower walls had burned first. Now they were beginning to collapse under the weight of the second story. Anyone trapped inside would be cinders by now.

Tying Copper at a safe distance, Matt covered the rest of the ground on foot. His gut churned as he raced closer. Men, women and horses, bathed in the hellish glow of the flames, milled in the yard. A bucket brigade had been formed from the cistern to the barn, but it was plain to see that if the roof caught fire from windblown sparks, nothing could be done. The air was rank with smoke. It filled Matt's lungs and burned his eyes as he searched the crowd for the one face he knew he wouldn't find.

Virgil Gates was standing in the ring of watchers, a dazed expression on his soot-streaked face. There was no sign of Lillian.

Catching his attention, Matt beckoned him aside. He had to raise his voice to be heard above the din of roaring flames and shouting men.

"What happened, Virgil? Where's Mrs. Gates?"

Raw-eyed, Virgil stared at the blazing house. "Lil's in there. She couldn't make it out, and I couldn't get to her. It was that little Hammond bitch that done it! She set the fire!"

"Did you see her do it?" Matt forced himself to speak calmly.

Virgil shook his head as he fumbled in his vest pocket. "I was in the barn. Heard the dog barking, came out and saw the fire. But I know it was her. I found this outside." He held up the leather pouch from the race, then thrust it into Matt's hand. "I recognized her in Sheridan when she won this, Marshal, and I saw you ride off to give it to her!"

Matt swallowed the leaden taste in his mouth. "Where's Miss Hammond now? Have you seen her?"

Again Virgil shook his head. "Fire started inside the house. Far as I know, she could be in there, too. Maybe the dog kept her from gettin' out. He's a mean son of a gun and he don't like strangers. That's why I bought him."

Matt turned away long enough to compose his features. Inside, he was all but screaming. Jessie couldn't have done this. And she couldn't be gone. His mind could not accept what he'd heard until he'd seen solid evidence.

But wasn't he holding that evidence in his hand right now? The leather pouch, with the five gold coins inside, was a sure sign that Jessie had been here. It didn't prove she'd started the fire, or that she'd been trapped in the burning house, but it led reason in that direction.

"I loved Lil, you know, Marshal," Virgil said, staring at the house. "I know it wasn't right, her bein' my brother's widow, but we meant to be married after her mourning was done."

"I'm sorry," Matt said, thinking of what he'd have to tell Virgil later. According to the message from St. Louis, Lillian had been wed three times before she met and married Allister. All of her husbands had been wealthy, and each one had died under suspicious circumstances. But no investigator had been able to pin the blame on the glamorous widow.

Lillian had almost surely killed Allister as well. The motive, means and opportunity had come together when Frank Hammond had fled the corral with the stallion, leaving his rifle behind. Jessie must have guessed as much. But burning down the house, killing the one person who could prove her brother's innocence, made no sense at all. Jessie wouldn't have started the fire, not unless it had been an accident.

Heartsick, Matt walked as close as he dared to the burning house. Heat seared his face, singeing his hair and eyebrows as he stared into the flames. The inside of the house was an inferno. Nothing could be alive in there.

But Lord, how could Jessie be gone? How could he not know it? How could he not feel it in the black emptiness of his soul?

Only as he backed away did he happen to glance

down. There on the concrete step of the portico was a small, instantly recognizable boot print.

The first thing Matt noticed about the print was that it was leading away from the front door, not toward it. Jessie could have been leaving when she'd left the track.

Dropping to a crouch, Matt looked closer. His breath stopped as he noticed something else.

The print of Jessie's thin, worn-out boot was etched in blood.

Jessie rounded the last bend in the road and saw, at last, the distant lights of the Tolliver Ranch. Pausing for a moment, she patted the mare's lathered side. "Almost there, girl! Then it's rest and oats for you!"

Straining her ears, she listened for the sound of galloping hoofbeats on the road behind her. She heard nothing except the wind whispering in the long prairie grass and the nighttime songs of crickets. Where were her pursuers? Had they given up? Had she finally lost them?

Nudging Gypsy to a trot, she headed for the light that glowed behind the windows of the rambling log house. Virgil's hired thugs would know better than to follow her to the ranch, Jessie told herself. There would be enough armed cowhands around the place to hold off a small army.

Knowing the Tollivers, she'd likely be offered a

good meal, a hot bath and a clean, soft bed, all of which she would gratefully accept. Her bitten leg, which was still oozing blood, would need to be cleaned and bandaged as well. But first she would sit down with Morgan Tolliver and tell him everything that had happened. If he had any reservations about taking her in, she would leave first thing in the morning.

As the light grew brighter and nearer, her thoughts returned to Matt. Would he guess that she was here and come to her? Or had he washed his hands of her once and for all?

One way or another, Matt would learn about the fire. He would hear the accusations that were bound to arise and, likely as not, he'd believe them. Why shouldn't he believe them? Why shouldn't everyone?

Heaven help her, she was in so much trouble. Maybe the smartest thing would be to disappear, leave the territory, change her name and make a new start someplace else. But right now she was hurt and exhausted, and her mare couldn't last another mile. Her plans for the future would have to wait until morning.

On closer approach, the ranch seemed unusually quiet. The bunkhouse was dark, the corral almost emptied of horses. It was branding time, Jessie realized. Most of the cowhands would be camped out on the range, rounding up the herds and branding the new calves before driving them up to summer pasture in the mountains.

In the house, lamps still burned in the curtained parlor. The hour was late, but not so late that everyone would have gone to bed. If Morgan was out with the branding crew, at least his wife might be home. At this hour she'd probably be reading or sewing, relaxing at the end of a long day.

Jessie hadn't visited the ranch since before her parents' death, so she'd never met the new Mrs. Tolliver. She could only hope Morgan had alerted his wife that she might be coming and that the woman wouldn't be put out by her presence.

A vague uneasiness prickled through her as she looped Gypsy's reins over the hitching rail and mounted the steps to the wide covered porch. The front door was closed. She rapped once, then again, her ears straining for an answer in the silence.

At last she heard a stirring from the parlor and the sound of light, rapid footsteps. The latch clicked and the door slowly opened.

The woman who stood in the dim entry, dressed in a simple blue gown, was only a little taller than Jessie herself. Her dainty features were enhanced by a tumble of dark red curls and expressive blue eyes—eyes that, Jessie realized suddenly, were wide with terror.

"You must be Jessie," she said in a taut whisper. "I'm Cassandra Tolliver. Please—come in."

Only as she crossed the threshold did Jessie see

the stocky shadow behind the door and catch the glimmer of lamplight on a gap-toothed grin. "'Bout time you showed up, girlie," said the man called Lem. "Ringo and me, we been waitin' for you."

Chapter Sixteen

The cold pistol jabbing against her ribs told Jessie that she'd made a fatal mistake. She could only guess that Virgil's hired guns had realized where she was going and taken some unknown shortcut to the ranch, planning to cut her off. Finding Morgan's wife alone, they'd decided to force their way into the house and take her hostage.

Cassandra walked back into the parlor. She moved like a puppet, her body rigid and trembling. Following her, Jessie saw the reason why.

Ringo sat in an armchair with his long legs crossed and his rifle balanced across one knee. Across the room, huddled on the settee, were three children—a girl of five or six with her mother's russet curls and a pair of younger twin boys with straight black hair and dark, frightened eyes. All three were dressed in their nightclothes. They looked rumpled and dazed, as if they'd just been rousted out of bed.

Cassandra sank onto the settee and caught her children close, protecting them with her body. Ringo grinned, his mouth splitting the ugly white scar that zigzagged down his face.

"Right pleased to see you, Miss Hammond. My friend and I have orders to arrest you and take you back to Felton as our prisoner."

"Arrest her?" Cassandra had recovered her spunk. "That's poppycock! You two aren't lawmen! What are you claiming she's done?"

"The charges," Ringo drawled, as if savoring each syllable, "are trespassing, arson and murder, namely the murder of Mrs. Lillian Gates."

"You've got it wrong." Jessie kept her eyes on Ringo, but her words were for Cassandra. "I admit to trespassing. But I didn't start the fire, and I certainly didn't murder anyone."

Ringo's skeletal grin widened. "That's not what Virgil says. You come on back to Felton with us now, Miss Hammond. I'm sure we can get this little misunderstanding cleared up in no time."

Jessie's gaze darted from the gunman to Morgan's wife, who was still huddled on the settee with her children. The Tollivers had offered her refuge and she had brought danger into their home. Whatever happened, she could not allow this precious family to be harmed.

Lem and Ringo would not be taking her back to Felton, she knew. They would have orders from Virgil to kill her and dump her body where it would never be found. But Cassandra and her children would be safer not knowing that. For their sake, she had to stage a show of bravery.

"Fine," she said, stepping toward the door. "Let's get back to Felton so I can tell my side of the story. I'm certain Marshal Sims will be very interested."

The two men exchanged startled glances. Clearly, they'd thought she would put up a fight, and they'd planned to control her by threatening Cassandra and the children. Now that would not be necessary.

Ignoring the guns, Jessie strode toward the entry hall. "Well, what are you waiting for?" she demanded, pausing in the doorway. "Let's get moving!"

She walked out to the porch. For the space of a heartbeat, she was tempted to make a break, run for her horse or dive into some hiding place. But that would leave the two gunmen alone with Morgan's family. She would not risk their safety for her own chance to escape.

Lem went off to get their mounts, which he'd hidden behind one of the sheds. Ringo kept the rifle on Jessie. His reptilian eyes watched her every move as she climbed onto her mare. Gypsy was worn out, but the other horses would be, too, she reminded herself. Wherever they were taking her, they wouldn't be able to hurry.

After Lem brought the horses around, he held his pistol on her while Ringo tied her hands behind her back. Jessie thought of Frank and the helplessness he must have felt as Matt cuffed his hands behind him. But she could no longer blame Matt for what had happened. He had only done what any lawman would do. It was her own interference, along with the sudden appearance of the vigilantes, that had triggered her brother's accident.

Strange, she thought, how things became clear when one was about to die.

The two men mounted up, flanking her closely on either side. Lem shot her a leering grin as they moved out of the yard and passed beneath the gate. Jessie looked straight ahead, her mind working frantically. How much time did she have left? Hours? Minutes? She would use that time to learn all she could. The more she knew about their plan, the better chance she'd have of escaping. Right now, only one thing was certain—she had nothing to lose.

"You know, that fire on the ranch is bound to ruin Virgil," she said. "You two boys probably won't even get paid for this job, especially if your boss ends up in jail. If I were in your shoes, I'd be on my way to greener pastures somewhere else."

There was a long breath of silence, in which the two men seemed to be digesting the fact that this woman wasn't going to cry and beg for mercy.

"We already talked about that," Lem said. "We'll be clearin' out afore long, maybe goin' to California. But first we's gonna have us a little farewell party— and you're invited, girlie." He snorted, spraying drops of moisture. "Invited, hell, you're gonna be the guest of honor!"

"Shut up, Lem," Ringo muttered. "You talk too much."

"Oh, no!" Jessie protested. "I like parties! Please, tell me more!"

Lem spat between the gap in his teeth. "Well, this friend of ours, Ike Holdaway, he's got a cabin up in these hills where we're headed. Only thing is, Ike don't need the cabin no more on account of he got sent up for bank robbery. An' he don't need the stash of whiskey jugs he left under the floor, neither. So me an' Ringo we figured with the cabin, the whiskey an' a purty little thing like you, we could have ourselves a real good time!"

Jessie suppressed a convulsive shudder. "And what about taking me back to Felton?" she asked innocently. "I'd like to tell my story to Marshal Sims."

"That can wait," Ringo growled. "Now stop yammering, you two, and let's ride!"

He nudged his horse to an easy trot. Jessie did the same, hoping the faster pace would leave deeper tracks, in case anyone tried to trail them.

But she wasn't optimistic about that. Morgan Tolliver was on the roundup, and Matt would have no way of knowing she was in trouble. He probably thought she was still on the mountain, right where he'd left her.

At least Lem and Ringo didn't plan to kill her right away, Jessie reminded herself. But if she couldn't get away from them, she would wish they had.

Matt had spent a frantic hour searching the Gates Ranch and the brushy land around it. He had torn through the outbuildings, circled the scrubby hills and waded between the willow-hung banks of the creek. Everywhere he'd looked, he'd imagined Jessie huddled there in the shadows, wounded, bleeding and terrified. But all the shadows had been empty. He had found no trace of her.

Focusing his thoughts, he tried to put himself in her place. Her cabin was hours away, and the mountains were treacherous at night. If she was scared and bleeding, where would she go to find safety?

Unless she had friends he wasn't aware of, there was just one likely answer.

Finding his horse, Matt sprang into the saddle and headed for the Tolliver Ranch at a gallop.

By the time he sighted the ranch house, the full moon had crested the sky and was slipping toward the western hills. Matt had not expected to find anyone awake at this hour, but the windows of the main house blazed with light. As he pounded through the gate, he recognized Morgan's roan tied to the hitching rail. A slight, dark young man was leading a sturdy bay out of the barn.

Matt reached the house and flung himself out of the saddle. Morgan had come out onto the porch, followed by a petite redhead that Matt guessed to be his wife. Clearly agitated, she was carrying a heavy cartridge belt.

"Jessie Hammond—is she here?" Matt demanded.

"She was." Morgan took the belt from his wife and buckled it around his lean hips. "You're just in time to help me go after her, Marshal."

"They took her," Morgan's wife broke in. "Two awful men, one with a missing tooth, and one with a scar, like this." She traced a zigzag line down her pretty face. "They called each other Lem and Ringo, and they said they were taking her back to Felton—" She shook her russet curls. "I'm sure Jessie knew that was a lie. She went willingly, Marshal, but I know it was only because she was afraid they'd hurt the children."

Matt swallowed stomach-curdling fear as the truth sank home.

"How long ago were they here?" he managed to ask.

"About three hours," Morgan said. "Cassandra sent Johnny up to the camp to fetch me. We got back here just a few minutes ago." He nodded toward the slim, dark young man who was shifting the saddle from the roan to the bay. "Get the Marshal a fresh horse, too, Johnny. He's going to need it."

"Right away." His pale face flashed in the darkness, and Matt was startled to see that his features were Chinese.

Morgan had noticed Matt's surprise. "Johnny's the son of Chang, our cook," he explained. "Best damned cowboy you ever saw. He'll make foreman one day if he stays around."

Ten minutes later they were ready to go. Johnny Chang, who would stay behind and guard the house, had brought Matt a deep-chested gray gelding and taken Copper to the barn. Judging from the angle of the stars, the time was close to two in the morning.

It would be a dangerous mission. At the top of the porch steps, Morgan caught his wife in his arms for a brief but passionate farewell kiss. Watching them from his horse, Matt made a silent vow. If he had to choose between preserving his own life or Morgan's, he would make sure this man returned whole and safe to his family.

Was Morgan his brother? The question flashed through Matt's mind as they rode away from the ranch and picked up the trail where the riders had left the wagon road. But the answer no longer mattered.

Right now, nothing mattered except finding Jessie and getting her safely back.

The cabin was small but solidly built, with thick log walls and a corrugated tin roof. Out back there was a privy. Lem freed Jessie's hands and held the pistol on her while she went inside to use it. The cramped space was filthy and infested with big cat-face spiders, but at least it offered some privacy.

In the darkness, she rolled up her pants leg and felt her calf where the dog had bitten her. The wound was caked with dried blood that had soaked her stocking and spread through the worn sole of her boot, but the oozing appeared to have stopped. The bite was the least of her worries, Jessie reminded herself as she came outside to a sky that was just beginning to fade in the east. Right now her captors were tired and hungry. This could be the best time to lull them into lowering their guard.

Lem did not retie her hands, but the pistol he jammed against her ribs was enough to keep her from running. From the front of the cabin Jessie heard the sound of splintering wood. Coming around the corner, she saw that Ringo had pried the padlocked hasp off the thick wooden door.

Inside, the cabin was as filthy as the privy had been. Half-eaten dishes of food moldered on the crude plank table, as if someone had left in the middle of a meal and never come back. The tabletop was littered with mouse droppings, the floor with bones and bottles. Jessie clenched her jaws to keep from gagging.

A bed with a ragged quilt and a dirty, bloodstained mattress stood in one corner. Unable to bear looking at it, Jessie turned back toward the kitchen. "I don't know about you boys, but I could do with some breakfast!" she declared. "There's not much to work with here, but I'll bet I could rustle us up some flapjacks!"

Lem's pale eyes widened expectantly, but Ringo wrinkled his nose in distaste. "I'd rather starve than eat anything in this pigsty," he growled. "All I want from here is a good drunk and a few pokes. After that, you'll be bound for the promised land, Miss Hammond. So you can drop that cheerful act. You're not fooling me." His head jerked toward Lem. "Help me tie the little bitch to the bed. Then we'll look for that whiskey!"

Jessie began to struggle as they grabbed her arms. Small as she was, she was fighting for her life, and it took both men to hold her. Ringo's thin fingers, as strong as steel wire, closed around her arm. Twisting sharply, she found the back of his hand with her mouth and bit down with all her strength. For an instant she tasted the hot spurt of his blood. Then his free hand struck her face in a slap so brutal that it nearly broke her jaw.

Jessie reeled backward. Lem caught her from behind, pinioning her arms while Ringo slapped her again. Blood from his bitten hand streamed down the front of his clean white shirt. "Try that again, bitch, and I'll kill you," he snarled.

The two men gagged Jessie with a bandanna and maneuvered her onto the bed, which was no more than a platform supported by wooden posts at each corner. Lashing her wrists together, they pulled her arms to the corner of the mattress, dropped the rope over the edge and knotted it around one sturdy wooden leg. Jessie's struggles only tightened the rough hemp around her wrists, making it dig into her flesh.

Hurting, she lay still while the two men pried up a floorboard and rummaged for the cache of whiskey. Lem's raucous whoop told her they'd found it.

How drunk would they be when they turned on her? Jessie could only lie on the filthy bed and will herself not to feel what they would do.

Dawn was a sliver of light above the prairie when Matt and Morgan spotted the cabin. Leaving their mounts downslope, they took their guns and crept upward on foot through the trees.

The hillside structure was built like a fort—solid log walls and high, narrow windows. With enough supplies, a man inside could hold off an army. Matt hoped to hell they wouldn't have to fight their way in.

Three horses were tethered nearby in the trees. One of them was Jessie's mare. Unless they'd already killed her, Jessie would be inside the cabin, scared, hurt and likely raped by the bastards as well. The thought of what they might have done made him want to charge the door, kick it in and shoot them full of bloody holes. But he'd come to save Jessie, he reminded himself. In an all-out gunfight, she would be the first to die.

"I know this place," Morgan whispered. "There's a window in back, and the land slopes up behind it. If you can distract them from the front, I'll go around and try to get the drop on them."

Matt nodded. "Be careful," he said. "If Jessie's in there, we don't want her hurt."

Morgan's black eyes flashed understanding. The fact that Jessie's mare was there didn't mean they'd find her alive. Until they knew either way, they would have to calculate every move.

Balancing his rifle, Morgan slipped through the aspens toward the rear of the cabin. He moved like an Indian, his boots barely stirring the leaves beneath his feet. As he disappeared from sight, Matt edged closer to within easy earshot of the cabin.

"This is Marshal Langtry!" he shouted. "We've come for the Hammond woman! She's all we want. Send her out alive, and you two can ride away from here!"

There was a moment of nerve-grinding silence before a cold, cultured voice answered.

"I hardly think that would be a good idea, Marshal. Miss Hammond here is our insurance. Let her go, and we'll have no guarantee you won't come after us."

"Let me know she's alive!" Matt shouted. "Then we'll talk!"

"And if she isn't?" The question cut into Matt like a blade.

"We've got the cabin surrounded," he retorted. "If you've killed Jessie Hammond, there won't be enough left of you and your friend to scrape off the walls."

"In that case, I can tell you that she's very much alive. But if you, and whoever's with you, aren't headed down that hill by the time I count to ten, she's not going to look as pretty as she does now."

Matt fought back dizzying rage. Emotion would only make him reckless, he reminded himself. "Prove she's in there, you bastard," he rasped. "Prove she's alive."

There was a brief hush, broken only by the sound of movement inside the cabin. Then the stillness was shattered by an agonized scream.

"Matt!"

The pain and terror in Jessie's voice almost undid Matt. It was all he could do to keep from rushing the cabin, his pistol blazing impotently against the solid wooden door.

The gunman would have more power now. He had heard Jessie cry out Matt's name, and he would know that she was not just another hostage. She was the woman Matt loved.

"Satisfied, Marshal?" The voice was cold as the sound of a rifle bullet sliding into the chamber. "I believe you know my terms. But I'm a fair man. I'll give you a choice. Which would you rather have my friend here cut off first, an ear or a finger?"

Matt forced himself to keep silent. Lord, where was Morgan? When would he make his move?

"No answer? Very well, Marshal, on the count of ten. One…two…three…"

Jessie lay immobilized on the bed. To keep her quiet while they were drinking, they'd tied her feet as well, and gagged her mouth, except for the few seconds when they'd let her cry out.

"Five…six…seven…" Ringo counted with the precision of a metronome while Lem pulled his knife out of its greasy leather sheath. He would cut off her ear, Jessie thought. With her hands bound, a finger would be more difficult to reach. She braced herself for the pain. Even if Matt left they would do it, just for the pleasure of hearing her scream.

Why hadn't she listened to Matt and gone down

the mountain with him? She'd done everything wrong. Now she'd be lucky to die fighting.

"Eight…nine…ten." Ringo glanced at Lem. "Do it," he said.

Lem ambled toward the bed. His right hand gripped the bone-handled knife. His left hand reached for the gag that covered Jessie's mouth.

The rifle shot, coming out of nowhere, was deafening in the closed space of the cabin. Lem's mouth dropped open in a rictus of death. Jessie glimpsed the crimson stain spreading across his chest as he staggered, then fell at the foot of the bed, shot cleanly through the heart.

With the reflexes of a rattlesnake, Ringo dived for the floor and rolled under the edge of the bed. For the moment, it was a smart move. The shooter at the back window, most likely Morgan Tolliver, wouldn't be able to reach him without hitting Jessie. But Ringo had dropped his rifle by the door. If he went for it, he would become a target.

"Jessie! Are you all right?" Matt shouted.

Jessie heard him, but the tight gag kept her from answering. She strained and twisted helplessly against the ropes. She could hear Ringo shifting under the bed. He would be after Lem's knife and pistol, she realized.

"It's over, you bastard!" Morgan's voice rang through the broken back window. "Give up now, or you'll be as dead as your friend!"

Ringo's reply was an obscenity so vile that it made Jessie shudder. She heard the scrape of metal against the floor and knew that he'd dragged the pistol out of Lem's holster. The slackening of the rope that tied her feet to the bed told her he'd found the knife as well.

Keeping low, he eased himself upward between the bed and the wall and jammed the pistol against Jessie's temple. "We're getting out of here, little lady," he rasped. "No tricks, or I'll blow that pretty head off."

She felt the sudden release as the knife freed her bound wrists from the bed. Then he was pulling her to her feet, using her body to shield him from Morgan's rifle at the rear window. Jessie resisted the urge to struggle. He would be taking her outside, she reminded herself. Matt and Morgan were there. Once Ringo was in the open, she would make her move and pray they could take him down.

Keeping his back to the wall, he dragged her toward the door. The tight ropes had cut off the blood supply to her feet. They tingled painfully as the feeling returned. Her stomach was queasy from the stench of the cabin and from her own fear.

"Back off!" Ringo yelled. "I've got a gun on the little lady and I'm coming out! Anybody moves, and she dies!"

His left arm hooked her throat. His right hand held the gun at her temple. With some awkward shifting, he slid back the bolt. Then, securing his grip on her, he kicked the door open with his boot.

They stepped out into the glare of the rising sun. Jessie's vision was nothing but a blur of white light. Ringo's, she suddenly realized, would be the same. She had to act now before his eyes adjusted to the brightness.

She'd read stories about ladies so delicate that they swooned at the sight of blood. Jessie had never swooned in her life, but it was the most sensible plan that came to mind.

Half expecting to die, she willed her body to go as limp as a hundred-pound sack of pinto beans.

Ringo was a man of wiry strength and Jessie was a small woman, but she'd caught him unprepared to support her dead weight. He swore as he sagged to the left, his gun hand instinctively flying outward to balance his body. As Jessie slid lower, Matt appeared through the trees in a blur of light.

Ringo's frantic shot went wild. Jessie heard the whine as it ricocheted off a boulder. Almost at the same instant, Matt fired. The bullet slammed solidly into Ringo's chest. Jessie rolled clear as he staggered, collapsed on his side and lay still.

Matt crossed the distance between them at a run. In the space of a heartbeat, Jessie was in his arms.

"I'm all right," she murmured as he ripped off the gag. He held her fiercely, kissing her hair, her forehead, her eyelids. "I'm all right, my love…"

Morgan came around the side of the cabin, his rifle balanced in his hand. A rare grin lit his stern Shoshone features as he saw Matt release Jessie. "I should have guessed about you two," he said. "Good shooting, by the way, Marshal."

Jessie would be haunted by the seconds that followed for the rest of her life.

As Morgan walked toward them, he noticed Lem's pistol, which had flown out of Ringo's hand and was lying on the ground a few feet from his body. Pausing with his back to the gunslinger, he bent down to pick it up.

Morgan didn't see the flutter of Ringo's eyelids or the movement of Ringo's hand, reaching down to draw a small but deadly derringer out of his boot and aim it at Morgan's back.

But Matt did.

"No!" Matt dived for the gun as Ringo's grip tightened on the trigger. He was still in the air when the tiny pistol fired.

The bullet caught Matt in the ribs, knocking him sideways. He rolled onto his back and lay still, blood flowing from beneath his leather vest.

Morgan's rifle shot ended the gunman's life, but Jessie scarcely heard it. With an anguished cry, she flew to Matt's side. Falling on her knees beside him, she groped for the awful wound and pressed it with her hands. As the blood flowed between her fingers, she crooned words of love and muttered desperate, incoherent prayers. So much blood. And his face was so pale.

"I love you, Matt," she whispered. "Don't die. Please, God, don't let him die."

Chapter Seventeen

Matt lay with his head in Jessie's lap, drifting in and out of consciousness. His skin was ashen, his pulse thready. The bullet had torn deep into his body. The wound neither bubbled like a lung shot nor gave off the gassy stench of gut penetration—Jessie thanked heaven for that. But the loss of blood was overwhelming. She had never seen so much blood.

Morgan, who'd spent his youth among his mother's people and knew something of their medicine, had packed the wound with a poultice of yarrow leaves and ripped his own shirt into strips to bind it in place. Now, racing with time, he felled several straight aspens to rig into an Indian-style travois.

While Morgan worked on the travois, Jessie cradled Matt's head, bathing his face and giving him sips of water from a canteen. Even the swallowing seemed to drain his strength, but he seemed to know how much his body needed fluids. He drank willingly.

As she held him, she whispered endearments, all the little love words she had ever wanted to say to him. And she told him about all the things that had happened to her since their parting on the mountain. "It was Lillian who killed Allister," she said at the end. "But everything else—Virgil, the fire, and *this*—" She glanced around the clearing where so much horror had taken place. "One way or another it was all set loose by my own reckless pride. And now, if I lose you for it—oh, Matt—"

Dry sobs choked off her words as she bent over him. She saw his lips move, but he was too weak to give voice to whatever he was thinking. Jessie could only pray that he would understand how sorry she was and how much she loved him.

When the travois was finished and lashed behind the gray horse, Jessie and Morgan used the quilt from the cabin to lift Matt onto it. The trip back to the ranch would be agony, but they had no hope of saving him here. Removing the bullet and cleaning the wound would require the skill of a doctor.

The trail down to the wagon road was so rocky that Morgan and Jessie had to walk behind the horse, carrying the foot of the travois to keep it from bumping on the ground. Matt lay with his eyes closed, saying nothing. But Jessie noticed the way his jaw clenched when the going was rough. He had to be in terrible pain.

The sun crawled upward as they wound their way out of the hills. By the time they reached the wagon road it was late morning. Morgan helped Jessie drag the travois into the shade of a cedar bush. Then he mounted Gypsy, the fastest horse they'd brought along, and made for the ranch at full gallop. He would send Johnny Chang flying to Sheridan for the doctor. Then he planned to return straightaway with the buckboard. In the meantime it would be up to Jessie to keep Matt alive.

She sat beside him as the shadows shrank and the day grew warmer. Morgan had left her with a full canteen. She used the water to wipe Matt's clammy skin and trickle between his bloodless lips. To keep him from drifting off, she talked to him, sang to him, kissed his cool, pale hands. Now and then his coppery eyes would flicker open to gaze up at her, or his fingers would tighten around hers. But Jessie didn't encourage him to speak. He needed all his strength just to keep from dying.

When Jessie's eyes weren't on Matt's face they wandered down the wagon road to where the twin ruts vanished around a scrubby hill. Where was Morgan now? Had he reached the ranch? Had he sent Johnny for the doctor? Was he on his way back with the wagon?

Jessie rose to her feet, shading her eyes to peer down the road. She'd expected Morgan long before this. What if something had happened to him? What if he wasn't coming back at all?

Two ravens circled against the hot blue sky, riding the updrafts on stiffened black wings. Jessie's Irish mother had always said that ravens were birds of death. Now, instinctively, Jessie bent over Matt's body, spreading her arms as if to cover him from sight. "They won't take you!" she muttered fiercely. "I won't let them! You're not going to die, Matthew Langtry!"

Inexplicably, her tears began to flow. Like drops of salty rain they fell on Matt's face, bathing him in her anguish. If only she could turn back time, she thought, to the moment when Ringo had reached for the derringer in his boot. Then she could have flung herself ahead of Matt and taken the bullet for him. She could be the one lying in agony on the travois, her life draining away drop by drop.

Moments later she glanced up to see the buckboard coming around the bend in the road, raising a plume of dust as it raced toward her. Weak with relief, she rose to her feet and began to wave.

Morgan had brought along Thomas Chang, Johnny's husky elder brother, who dressed in Chinese clothes and wore his hair in the traditional pigtail. Using the quilt, Thomas and Morgan lifted Matt onto the mattress they'd laid in the buckboard to cushion the ride. Jessie clambered up beside him, and seconds later they were off.

For Jessie, the rest of the day, and the night that followed, passed in a blur. Cassandra came running out of the house to meet them, fluttering like an anxious mother bird as they carried Matt into the ground-floor guest room and laid him in the massive bed that had once been Jacob Tolliver's.

As they waited for the doctor, Thomas spooned cupfuls of exotic-smelling Chinese tea down Matt's throat. The tea seemed to ease his pain, but Jessie could not forget the bullet that had ripped into his body—the bullet that would have to be removed if Matt was to live.

Morgan, Cassandra and Thomas Chang drifted in and out of the room. Once, the doll-like Mei Li, mother of the two Chang boys, tottered in on her tiny bound feet with a pot of her medicinal tea. Even the Tolliver children peeked around the door frame to steal a forbidden glance at their visitors. Jessie paid them little heed. For her, nothing existed but the long, lean body in the bed, the ashen face, the closed eyelids and the hands that gripped hers in pain and trust.

Jessie had never imagined that she could love someone so much.

It was evening by the time the doctor arrived. He was middle-aged and portly, with close-cropped hair and sausage-shaped fingers that looked more like a butcher's than a surgeon's. But his hands proved to be strong and steady.

Even during the operation, Jessie refused to leave the room. She hovered by the bed as Matt was sedated with chloroform and propped on his side with pillows. Then she gripped his hands while the doctor probed for the bullet.

Even under sedation, Matt groaned as the long forceps inched deeper. The pain seemed to jolt through his hands and into Jessie, so that she felt it as her own. Tears squeezed from beneath her eyelids and trickled down her cheeks. She prayed silently that God would guide the doctor's hand.

Matt's body jerked reflexively as the forceps touched metal. "Found it," the doctor grunted. "It's deep. Another half inch and it would have lodged in his spine. He's a damned lucky man."

Removing the bullet was a delicate process. Sweat beaded on the doctor's forehead as he worked the forceps out of the wound. Jessie held her breath, gripping Matt's hands with all her strength.

An eternity seemed to pass before the doctor put down the forceps and held up the ugly, blood-coated ball of lead that had almost taken Matt's life. Then he cleaned the wound, dressed it with fresh wrappings and pronounced the operation finished.

"You look like you could use some sleep," he said.

"Get it while you can. Your young man won't be awake for hours."

Jessie shook her head. "I don't want to leave him. If I need to sleep I'll do it right here in this chair."

"All right. But first we need to take a look at that leg of yours."

After cleaning and bandaging Jessie's bitten leg, the doctor left the room to wash up. Cassandra had prepared a meal and a room for him. He would stay until dawn, then check on Matt again before driving his buggy back to Sheridan.

Jessie was slumped in the chair next to Matt's bed when Morgan's wife entered carrying a tray. "The doctor told me you wanted to stay in here," she said with a tired smile. "But I was hoping you'd at least take some supper."

Jessie stirred and sat up. "What time is it?" she muttered.

"It's almost nine. If you change your mind, there's a bed waiting for you, and a bath if you'd like one." Cassandra placed the tray on Jessie's lap. The hot beef stew, buttered bread and cold milk looked delicious.

Jessie murmured her thanks and began to eat. She was ravenously hungry, but almost too exhausted to chew.

Cassandra moved a straight-backed chair close to the foot of the bed and sat down, facing Jessie. Now that Morgan's wife was no longer terrified, she looked prettier than ever. Her soft auburn curls framed a delicate face and sparkling cornflower eyes. When she glanced toward the lamp, its light revealed a trail of freckles across her pert nose.

"I left some clothes in your room. The dresses haven't fit me since the twins were born, so you're welcome to keep them."

"You're very kind to me, especially after all the trouble I caused you. I could have gotten your whole family killed."

Cassandra shook her head. "Don't punish yourself, Jessie. I'm very aware of what you did for us last night, leaving with those men, getting them out of the house so they wouldn't hurt the children. You're a brave woman."

"And then I almost got Morgan shot, too. He could have been the one lying here, or maybe worse, if Matt hadn't—"

"I know." Cassandra reached across the corner of the bed and laid a hand on Jessie's knee. "Morgan told me how Matt took the bullet for him. All we can do now is be thankful he wasn't killed."

Jessie stared down at her hands, fighting tears.

"You must love him a great deal," Cassandra said softly.

"I do. But I've been such a reckless fool. What if he won't forgive me?"

"I can't imagine that happening, my dear." Cassandra rose to her feet. "If you're determined to stay here with him, I'll bring you a quilt and a pillow. Is there anything else you need?"

"Thank you, not a thing. You've already done so much, I— Wait! There is something! I'll need to write a note to the sheriff so the doctor can take it to Sheridan tomorrow."

"You'll find paper, pens and ink in that desk next to the window. But for heaven's sake, get some rest, Jessie, before the doctor ends up with two patients on his hands instead of one!"

"I will," Jessie promised, using the bread to sop up the last morsel of delicious stew. "But first I need to write down what happened. If I go to sleep, I might forget something."

After Cassandra had bustled out with the tray, Jessie sat down at Jacob Tolliver's desk and began to write. The pen scratched furiously away, one page, then two, then three. She could only pray that the sheriff would believe her. Even after what she'd witnessed it would be her word against Virgil's. But this time she would have two powerful allies, Matt and Morgan.

By the time she'd finished her letter, Jessie was drained of strength and emotion. Matt had not stirred, but his breathing was deep and regular, and the color was returning to his skin. God willing, he would recover.

For a long time she stood looking down at him,

her eyes tracing the fine, strong features of his face. What a good man he was, like a white knight in one of her old storybooks, standing firm for truth and justice. Her conduct toward him had been erratic and treacherous at every turn, but Matt had never played her false. If she could be his, she would count every day of her life as a blessing.

When Matt opened his eyes the next morning, the first thing he saw was Jessie, sitting in the chair beside the bed. Her eyes were bloodshot and rimmed with deep shadows. Her hair was matted on one side, and there was an ugly purple bruise along her jaw. Her dirty, rumpled plaid shirt and denims looked as if she'd spent the night in them, which she likely had.

To him, she had never looked more beautiful.

With effort, he pieced the fragments of the past twenty-four hours into memory. Although some memories were lost in a dark fog, one certainty was that she had been with him the whole time. He remembered her touch, her voice, her spirit strengthening his will to live.

He had been laid on his right side and propped with pillows. Beneath him, his arm had lost all feeling. He struggled to turn himself and felt a jab of pain. He groaned.

Jessie laid a restraining hand on his shoulder. "No,

don't try to move yet. Wait for the doctor. He'll be here before long."

Matt forced his lips to shape the words. "I don't suppose you'd care to join me in this bed…" he muttered. "I could use some company."

A smile lit her face. "Not yet," she whispered. "But soon, my love. Very soon."

They were clasping hands when the doctor walked in. The first thing he did was to shoo Jessie out of the room. "Get some breakfast and some honest-to-goodness rest. That's an order, young lady."

When Jessie had gone, the doctor changed Matt's dressing and observed that the flesh around the wound looked healthy. The husky, silent Chinese youth who'd come into the room helped maneuver Matt into a sitting position and propped him up with pillows.

The doctor closed his medical bag. "You're looking better, but you've lost a lot of blood," he said. "You're to stay right down for the next few days. I don't want you passing out and opening up that wound. Thomas, here, will see to your needs. He took care of Jacob Tolliver before the old man passed away, and he's a fine nurse. This is Jacob's old room, incidentally. I believe he died in this very bed."

Matt had resolved to forget any possible connection to the Tolliver family. But the doctor's words triggered a tightness in his chest that refused to go away. It was still there an hour later after Thomas had taken away his breakfast and brought a steaming wet washcloth for his face and hands. And the feeling only worsened a few minutes later, when Morgan walked into the room.

"How are you this morning?" he asked, settling into the armchair by the bed.

"Sore as blazes. And I'm afraid you'll be stuck with me for the next few days. Sorry I can't make myself useful while I'm here."

"We're just happy not to be digging your grave this morning," Morgan replied. "You saved my life when you took that bullet. I want to thank you for that—and to share something I've been saving for a while. This is as good a time as any."

He slipped an opened envelope out of his vest and held it toward Matt. "Read this," he said. "Take your time. It's from someone you know."

The tightness in Matt's chest increased as he took the envelope in his hand. His heart turned over as he stared at the return address. It was from Hamilton Crawford, the retired Pinkerton man he'd hired to investigate the Tollivers—and it was addressed to Morgan.

With shaking fingers, Matt withdrew the two-page letter from the envelope and began to read.

Dear Morgan,
Some business has recently fallen into my hands, the nature of which puts me in a diffi-

cult position. After long and careful thought, I have decided to contact you and to leave the matter in your hands.

A few days ago, my services were retained by a young man, one U.S. Deputy Marshal Matthew Tolliver Langtry. He was desirous of having me look into his possible relationship to your family. The marshal was born in Texas on April 7, 1859, to a young unmarried woman named Sally Langtry, now deceased. His only clue to the identity of his father is his middle name. He has assured me that even if a relationship can be proved, he wants nothing in the way of money, property or recognition. He simply seeks to know whether Jacob might have been his father.

I confess to a twinge of guilt when I accepted the young marshal's retainer. But I was not ready to tell him the truth—that I had known your family for years and that Jacob Tolliver had been one of my closest friends.

It is in the spirit of that friendship that I break a confidence and reveal a secret your father told me many years ago...

Matt felt Morgan's eyes on him, but he could not bring himself to look up. The tightness crept into his throat, almost choking him, as he read the rest of the letter.

You were a youth and your brother Ryan a small boy in the summer of 1858 when your father went to Texas to buy cattle and drive them home. You may remember him saying that he fell sick with fever in Texas. What I'm certain he didn't tell you is that he was taken in by a kindhearted young woman who nursed him back to health. She was sweet and pretty, and he came to care deeply for her. By the time he was well enough to leave, Jacob had betrayed his marriage vows.

Your father's family meant the world to him. He felt he had no choice except to end the love affair and return to Wyoming as if nothing had happened. He could only hope that, in due time, Sally, as he called her, would marry and find her own happiness.

Jacob never told me Sally's last name, but if I didn't feel certain that Matt Langtry was his son, I wouldn't be sending you this letter. When you set eyes on him, I have no doubt you'll agree. He's the very image of your father as a young man.

What happens now is up to you and your

family. If you choose to keep your father's secret, I'll tell the marshal I learned nothing and return his retainer, which I would do in any case. Either way, I will respect your wishes in this matter.

Sincerest regards,

Hamilton Crawford, Esq.

Lowering the letter, Matt stared at his brother. "You knew," he whispered hoarsely. "Even when you introduced yourself at the Gates funeral—you knew all along."

Morgan nodded slowly. "Forgive me. I needed time to make up my mind. I needed to discover what kind of man you were."

"There's nothing I expect from you," Matt said. "I want no part of the property your father left. And I certainly don't plan to change my name or do anything else to betray the secret. I only ask that you let me tell Jessie, and perhaps our children someday, when they're grown."

"That's fine. Cassandra knows. And Ham Crawford, of course. But no one else." Morgan shifted in his chair. "That brings me to another dilemma."

"Your brother Ryan," Matt guessed, and Morgan nodded.

"I was a boy when my own mother died. But when Jacob met your mother in Texas, he was married to

Ryan's mother, Ann Marie. She was a fine woman, and we always believed our father was faithful to her. I honestly don't know how Ryan is going to take this."

"Then maybe you shouldn't tell him. I'd like to meet Ryan someday, but I'd never approach him on my own. If the truth would hurt your brother, there's no reason for him to know about me."

Morgan scowled. "I'll think on it awhile. There's time. Ryan only visits us once or twice a year." Rising to his feet, he reached into his vest pocket. "For now, the most important thing is for you to rest and get well. But before I get back to the roundup, there's something I want to show you. I found it after Jacob died, when I was cleaning out his desk. You may or may not recognize it. If you do, it's yours."

He held out his hand. In his palm was a tarnished, heart-shaped brass locket. "Open it," he said.

Matt's fingers fumbled with the delicate catch. At last the little heart sprang open. The photograph inside, carefully trimmed to fit, was murky with age. But as Matt stared down at it, the tightness in his throat burst in a release so powerful that he almost wept.

Struggling, he found his voice. "I've never had a picture of my mother, except in my mind. You've given me…a missing piece of myself. Thank you."

Morgan muttered an acknowledgment. Clearly he was a man who kept his feelings under tight rein and felt uneasy in the presence of so much emotion. But when he glanced past Matt, toward the door, his face broke into a smile. "I see you have another visitor," he said. "I'll leave you two alone and get back to the branding. Oh—and I've sent Johnny up the mountain to fetch Jessie's old pinto. She'll be relieved to hear that, won't you, Jessie?"

Morgan stepped out of the room. Murmuring her thanks, Jessie passed him in the doorway. Matt's heart stopped at the sight of her. She had bathed and changed into an airy yellow gown with a heart-shaped neckline and a green sash drawn tight around her hand-span waist. Her hair lay in damp curls around her glowing face. She smiled as she floated toward the bed.

Matt grinned back at her, his heart overflowing. For the past twenty years he'd wandered alone. Now at last he felt as if he'd come home. Home to Jessie.

"Why, you clean up right nicely, Miss Hammond," he drawled. Then in a more serious tone he added, "Come and sit down, love. I've got something to show you…and something to ask you."

Epilogue

April, 1888

Matt and Jessie knelt in the straw gazing at Gypsy's newborn foal. Black like its sire, the velvety little creature was struggling to stand for the first time.

"Come on, baby," Jessie coaxed. "That's it. Feet underneath—oops! Come on…" She laughed as all four legs went sprawling.

The next attempt went better. With Gypsy's nuzzling encouragement, the foal staggered to its feet and stood quivering on impossibly long legs. Then it tottered to its mother and began to nurse.

Jessie's hand stole into Matt's. "He's magnificent," she whispered. "How I wish Frank could have seen him! This was his dream!"

Matt's fingers tightened around hers. "Now it's

our dream, too. And who's to say Frank isn't some-where close by, sharing it with us?"

Frank could rest in peace now, Matt hoped. Virgil Gates had backed up Jessie's story that Lillian had shot Allister, clearing Frank of all blame. Since it couldn't be proved that Virgil had murdered Lillian or that he'd ordered his thugs to track Jessie down and kill her, Virgil had gone free. But the trial had cost him money, friends and influence. Soon after, he'd sold his land, paid off his creditors and left the territory a broken man.

Matt and Jessie had bought their ranch, in the hills west of Sheridan, right after their wedding. For a time Matt had kept his marshal's job, but he'd soon discovered that his heart was in the land. This was where he belonged.

The ranch was not large. But they had room for a few hundred head of cattle, and for the horses that Jessie bred and broke. The black stallion would re-main free in the mountains, but his fiery lineage would continue in the foals that were born on the ranch. This one, Gypsy's colt, promised to be the most splendid horse of all.

"Your turn next." Matt patted Jessie's tautly bulg-ing belly. Laughing, she rubbed her head against his shoulder. Both of them wanted a big family. Heaven willing, their children would have a wonderful place to grow up, with two parents who loved them and each other. Matt felt contentment to the marrow of his bones.

Their relationship with Morgan's family was warm and friendly, even though their busy lives, and the decision to keep their shared blood a secret, limited the amount of time they spent together. It was enough, Matt told himself. He knew where he'd come from. He knew that Jacob Tolliver had loved his mother and he understood why Jacob had left her. It was all he'd ever wanted. Wasn't it?

"Matt!" Jessie's anxious voice broke into his musings. "I hear a horse outside, by the gate. We must have company."

Rising to his feet, Matt strode outside, with Jessie behind him. His sun-dazzled eyes made out the figure of a solitary rider coming into the yard.

As his vision cleared, Matt could see that the man was a total stranger. Clad in buckskins, he was tall and fair, with sun-streaked locks and a well-trimmed beard. He was mounted on the most beautiful Appaloosa horse Matt had ever seen.

Matt had never set eyes on the man—surely he would remember if he had. But as he stranger dismounted, swinging off his horse with the grace of a cougar, Matt felt an oddly familiar tightening around his chest.

"Matthew Langtry?" The stranger's voice was deep and rich.

"Yes," Matt replied cordially. "What can I do for you."

The stranger took a step toward him. Matt extended his hand, but the man did not take it. Instead he simply opened his arms. The grin on his face would have lit up an ocean of darkness.

"Ryan Tolliver," he said. "I'm your brother!"

* * * * *

Harlequin® Historical
Historical Romantic Adventure!

A game of chance is never
as exciting as the game of love!

THE DUKE'S GAMBLE
Miranda Jarrett

Eliot Fitzharding, Duke of Guilford,
visits Penny House to flirt with
Miss Amariah Penny, the gaming
den's proprietress. When the club
is accused of harboring a cheat,
Guilford and Amariah race to quash
the rumors. But they risk becoming
an item of choice gossip themselves!

Linked to RAKE'S WAGER #740
and THE LADY'S HAZARD #779

A *Penny House* Novel

On sale April 2006
Available wherever
Harlequin books are sold.